THE 1990s

Families

1990s

1980s

1970s

1960s

1950s

1940s

1930s

1920s

1910s

1900s

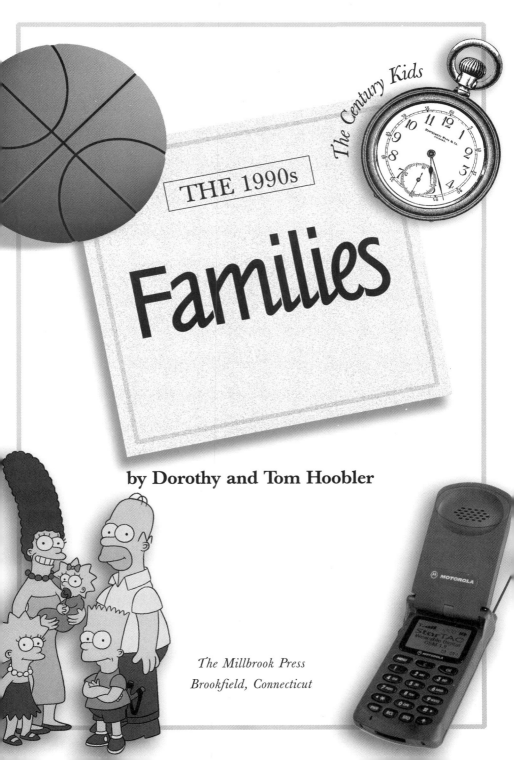

The Century Kids

THE 1990s

Families

by **Dorothy and Tom Hoobler**

The Millbrook Press
Brookfield, Connecticut

Photographs courtesy of PhotoEdit: pp. 6 (© Tony Freeman), 26
(© Myrleen Cate), 34 (© Bonnie Kamin), 44 (© Mary Kate Denny),
46 (© David Young-Wolff), 56 (© Robert Ginn), 57 (© Mark
Richards), 110 (© Bill Aron), 133 (© Gary Conner), 138 (© Jeff
Greenberg); H. Armstrong Roberts: p. 12 (© D. Logan); Getty Images:
p. 13 (© Byron Cohen); AP/Wide World Photos: pp. 16, 81, 96;
© Ford Motor Company: p. 19; International Stock: p. 20 (© Giovanni
Lunardi); Super Stock: pp. 21, 40; Bison Archives: p. 71; Photofest:
p. 115 (TM and © Twentieth Century Fox Film Corporation 1990);
Anne Canevari Green: p. 117; Corbis: p. 132 (© Bozi); IBM
Corporate Archives: p. 141

To everybody who read
all the other nine Century Kids
books–this one's for you!

Library of Congress Cataloging-in-Publication Data
Hoobler, Dorothy.
The 1990s : families / by Dorothy and Tom Hoobler.
p. cm.–(Century kids)
Summary: The Aldrich, Vivanti, and Dixon families gather to
celebrate Nell and Rocco's one hundredth birthdays as the
new century dawns and the specter of the Y2K bug threatens.
ISBN 0-7613-1609-4 (lib. binding)
[1. Year 2000 date conversion (Computer systems)–Fiction.
2. Family–Fiction.]   I. Hoobler, Thomas.   II. Title.
PZ7.H76227 Aaj 2002
[Fic]–dc21   2001007690

Published by The Millbrook Press, Inc.
2 Old New Milford Road
Brookfield, Connecticut 06804
www.millbrookpress.com

The Game

DECEMBER 19, 1999

THE BLUE KNIGHTS SPREAD OUT, COVERING MORE territory. But that only increased the space between them, giving room for an attacker to break through.

Cal wished he had more knights, but he hadn't found enough gold coins in the monastery wine cellar to buy them with. He had to use some of his hoard to shore up the breach in the south wall of his castle. Probably Moon Maiden had found the cache before he did. She had been under the lightning-split oak when the white owl revealed the hiding place.

Cal

And of course Cal's magician was now asleep because Cal hadn't figured out how to decipher the spell that would keep him awake.

Worst of all, Sir Roger was preparing to attack Cal's domain. That was obvious. Roger had been moving his forces to the border for at least a week. Roger was a clever opponent. Cal had lost some land to him a few months ago and ever since then, Roger had been looking for an opportunity to slice off some more.

Cal realized that he had to make an alliance with somebody. But then he'd have to trade something in return. He had some extra serfs, but nobody wanted them. They paid taxes too slowly and just gave Cal more people to defend in case of a domain invasion.

Cal typed in the code that brought up a list of currently online rulers who were near his domain. Three of them. Sir Roger, of course. Didn't he ever sleep? And Moon Maiden, who always wanted much more in tribute than her alliance was worth. Finally, Almanac. He was a fairly new player in The Game. Cal hadn't dealt with him before. Scouting him showed that he played a conservative, very slow game. But maybe he was ready to make an alliance.

Cal sent a courier to ask Almanac for a conference. After a moment, Almanac opened a communications box and got right to the point:

> ALMANAC: My scouts see that you are in danger of an attack by Sir Roger.
>
> BLAISE: I fear so too.

Like all the other players in The Game, Cal tried to sound like a medieval ruler when he communicated.

> ALMANAC: So I assume you have called to seek my help.
>
> BLAISE: That is so. I admit it.
>
> ALMANAC: What would you ask of me?
>
> BLAISE: I think that six knights and twelve archers will be sufficient.

A long pause. Cal became nervous as he watched the screen, waiting for an answer.

> ALMANAC: But you have little to offer me in return. I sense that your stock of gold coins has been depleted. And food? Your granaries hardly have enough to feed your villagers and warriors for another five days. Before then, you'll have to replenish them.
>
> BLAISE: I have land. I could trade you as much as 100 hectares in my northwest quadrant.

> ALMANAC: That is empty land, a nuisance to defend. It would need towns, mills, craft shops, and farms to be worth anything to me. Besides, I cannot spare the knights and archers you require.

Cal was annoyed. This meeting was just a waste of time.

> BLAISE: I see our discussion has been pointless. Perhaps we will meet again.
>
> ALMANAC: Stay a moment. I have another proposal. Suppose I launch my own attack on Sir Roger's domain. Then when he moves his forces to defend, you follow with an attack on the other side. Surely he'll be surprised.

That was true, Cal thought. It was a great idea. But there must be a catch.

> BLAISE: What would you want in return for this action?
>
> ALMANAC: First, any land and improvements that we capture from Sir Roger must be divided equally.
>
> BLAISE: Agreed.

That was a more generous offer than Cal had expected.

> ALMANAC: And one more favor.

Here comes the catch, Cal thought.

ALMANAC: You must tell me your name.

BLAISE: My name? It's on the screen.

ALMANAC: I mean your real name.

Cal smiled. Almanac would be surprised.

BLAISE: My screen name is my real name.

ALMANAC: Your real name is Blaise?

BLAISE: Blaise Pascal.

ALMANAC: He was a 17th-century philosopher.

BLAISE: And also the inventor of the first digital calculator. I was named after him.

ALMANAC: I see. So Pascal is not really your last name.

BLAISE: Right.

ALMANAC: But you must give me your full name. That's the agreement.

BLAISE: Why?

Everybody always said you shouldn't give your real name online. But why not? If this guy was some kind of stalker, he could do it online, since Cal was here several times a day. And as for real life, how could he ever find Cal? Even his parents' phone number was unlisted.

ALMANAC: I like to collect people's names.

Well, Almanac was a nut for sure, thought Cal.
But if Almanac would attack Sir Roger, Cal didn't
care.

BLAISE: This is all you want? After that, you'll
attack Sir Roger?

ALMANAC: The attack will begin at 8:05 P.M. Wait
until he moves his forces, and you can follow.
Will you be ready by then?

BLAISE: I'll be ready.

ALMANAC: So?

BLAISE: McShane. My full name is Blaise Pascal
Aldrich McShane.

ALMANAC: Nice to meet you, Cal.

It wasn't until after Almanac left that Cal wondered how he knew everybody called him Cal for
short.

T W O

Y2K

DECEMBER 20, 1999

JEN LOOKED OUT HER WINDOW TO WHERE THE tennis court was. Or where it used to be. All summer long, workers with backhoes had dug it up. The earth had been replaced now, but it was bumpy and rough. Jen couldn't have her friends over to play tennis there.

Of course there was a good reason for all this. Daddy had wanted to save them from the Y2K disaster, and he'd built a shelter underneath the tennis court.

The shelter would be like a clubhouse, Mom had told Jen and her little brother Cal. Jen knew Mom was just trying to make her and Cal think

Y2K was going to be fun. Jen had seen the inside of the shelter, however, and didn't like the idea of staying down there for very long.

But according to Daddy, it might be weeks, or even months. And he should know. He'd been warning people even before anybody called it Y2K, and he said it would be the biggest disaster of all time.

Anybody who wasn't ready for Y2K, according to Daddy, was either going to starve or freeze or be caught in an immense traffic jam. Or endure some other fate that was so horrible nobody'd even thought of it yet.

Unless you were prepared, that is. Which was why there was now a shelter underneath the tennis court. And why there was a tank with 10,000 gallons of gasoline connected to an electric generator in another part of the yard. Not to mention the dozens of boxes with dried and canned food that had been delivered a month ago. And the water pump that could be used by hand if necessary. Jen had already tried it. It took ten minutes for her to pump enough water to fill a glass.

Jen

This all seemed wrong, she thought. Jennifer couldn't imagine what it would be like not to be able to drive to the mall and fill the SUV with anything you wanted. Or what it would be like if the TV didn't work when you turned it on. No more Buffy? No way!

But Daddy should know. People listened to him. He was on TV a lot, and twice even went to Washington to testify before Congress.

Most people believed him, it seemed to Jen. That was partly because he knew so much about computers. He was the founder of the McByte

Buffy the Vampire Slayer

Company, which made the most popular computer software in the world. (And which had made *him* the ninth-richest person in the world. He never bothered to tell his children that. Jen had read it in *Forbes* magazine.)

Software was what caused the Y2K problem. Not McByte software, of course. No, way back when computers were new, people used two numbers for the year, like 55 instead of 1955. It was to save space in the computer's memory. Nobody seemed to realize, or care, that someday there would be a year 2055 or a 2155. That was too far in the future to worry about.

But on January 1, the year would be 2000—or, for short, Y2K. And all the computers would think it was the year 1900, because all they could understand was that it was the year 00.

And if a computer doesn't understand something, it crashes, as everybody who ever used a computer knows. (Even computers that used McByte software. That's just the way computers *were*, Daddy said.)

What made that a big problem was the fact that computers ran just about everything. Jen's little brother Cal said it was like a science-fiction story he'd read in which robots took over the world.

Only in real life, computers ran the electric generators, and if they turned off, so would everything from traffic lights to the big pumps that sent water into people's houses. And of course TV stations too.

Once, after Daddy returned from one of his trips warning people, Jen had an idea. "Why don't they just take the computers out of the electricity plants and let *people* turn the switches on and off?" she asked.

"Oh, you can't do that," said Daddy.

"Why not?"

"Because it's too difficult to run big plants like that without computers," he told her.

Jen wondered how people got their electricity *before* there were computers. But she supposed that was just something else that was too hard for her to understand.

It wasn't easy having a father who was probably the smartest person in the world (as well as the ninth richest). Jen studied hard, trying to learn as much about computers as she could. She was pretty good for a twelve year old, much better than anybody else in her class at the private school she went to. But those kids figured they were so rich they didn't have to learn anything.

The thing was, Jen felt she could never catch up with Daddy, no matter how hard she studied.

So it was a surprise to her when she found out that some people didn't think Daddy was right about Y2K. As January 1 drew nearer, there were still a lot of people who hadn't made preparations.

Maybe it wasn't possible for everybody to build a shelter in their backyard with its own electric generator. But everybody should have stocked up on bottles of water and canned food—and firewood, if they lived in cold places—to last for at least a month. "Six months to a year would be safest," Daddy said.

Daddy worried a lot about those people. But the one who bothered him the most was his stepmother, Nell.

A Florida woman poses with her Y2K emergency supplies.

Nell was really Daddy's cousin, twice removed or something like that. But when Daddy was a boy his real parents couldn't take care of him, so Nell raised him in her house. An old house in Maine—not the one she lived in now, in Beverly Hills, about two hundred miles down the Pacific coast from where Jen's family lived.

Nell was going to celebrate her one-hundredth birthday on January 1, the same day the big Y2K disaster was going to happen. And by a strange coincidence, so was Mom's grandfather Rocco, who was married to Nell.

Jen had been four when Nell and Rocco got married. She had been the flower girl at their wedding. At the time, she was too young to understand, but now she thought it was the most romantic story in the world. Nell and Rocco had known each other as children and then had been separated. Nell became a movie star, while Rocco opened a restaurant.

Then, years and years later, Rocco's granddaughter (who was Jen's mom) married Nell's adopted son (Daddy). That had brought Nell and Rocco together again, and since Rocco's first wife had died, one thing led to another. . . . They had moved out here to Nell's California beach house a few years ago because Rocco didn't like the cold weather in Maine.

So since their birthdays were both going to be on the same day—the day Daddy called "the most

dangerous day in the last two thousand years"—
Daddy thought they should come stay in *his*
house, where they'd be safe.

But Nell said no. She was one of those people
who didn't listen to reason, according to Daddy.
She said she and Rocco were going to celebrate
their birthdays in their own house, and all their
friends and relatives were invited to join them.

Ever since, Daddy had been trying to think up
a way to get Nell to change her mind. He even had
Mama try to persuade Rocco to come stay with
them. Daddy thought Nell would certainly follow.
But Rocco was loyal; if Nell was staying at their
beach house, so would he. (Secretly, Jen thought
that was kind of sweet.)

Daddy didn't give up, of course. Jen thought
he might be even more stubborn than Nell. She
was nearly a hundred, of course, and Jen couldn't
image what that felt like. Maybe getting old made
you more stubborn.

Jen sat up as she saw something else appear
outside the window. It was a brand-new sports car,
a Mustang convertible. Even if Jen hadn't known
the person driving it, she would have recognized
her by the color of the car. It was a certain shade
of blue-green that had been created especially for
one person.

Aunt Isabel.

A Mustang convertible

A cosmetics company had used that very same color in a series of ads that featured the famous model Isabel Viva. Isabel was Mama's sister. Her last name used to be Vivanti, but she changed it when she went into modeling.

Jen hopped up, leaned out the window, and waved. "Aunt Isabel! What are you doing here?"

That was a silly question, since Isabel was liable to drop in at the most unexpected times. She liked to travel and had friends all over the world. In fact, there was hardly anyplace she could go where people wouldn't recognize her.

Isabel

"I just got back from Africa," Isabel called. "I have something to tell your father. And you too."

"I'll be right down," said Jen. She changed into a T-shirt Aunt Isabel had given her. It was the same blue-green color as the Mustang and had the logo of the cosmetics company on it.

By the time Jen got downstairs, Mama was there greeting Isabel. It always seemed a little strange for Jen to see the two of them up close. Though they looked like sisters, there was something about Isabel that was scary. Oh, she was a nice person, but she was so beautiful you could hardly believe she was real. Jen felt a little sorry for Mama, having a sister who looked like that.

But Mama never seemed to mind. She and Isabel were already laughing about some joke that the two of them remembered from their childhood. Jen always thought that growing up in a restaurant must have been more fun than being the daughter of the ninth-richest man in the world.

"Sam sent you an e-mail a few weeks ago," Mama said. "A warning about Y2K. He was annoyed when you didn't reply."

"Well, believe it or not, I don't carry a laptop everywhere I go," Isabel replied. "And even more amazingly, there weren't many computers at all in the part of the world where I've been."

"Come inside and tell us all about it," said Mama. "We're just going to have lunch."

They sat down in the sunroom where Mama grew orchids. Even though the weather lately had been cold—for California—many of them were flowering. The orchids never seemed to stop, no matter what time of year it was.

Tran, their cook, was setting out brightly colored bowls around the glass-topped table. He nearly dropped one when he saw Isabel. With a cry, he rushed forward to hug her. Tran was pretty much a member of the family. When he had first arrived in the United States from Vietnam, Mama said, he could hardly speak English. Now he read through Jen's papers for school, marking corrections even before her teacher could.

Tran

Tran's big ambition was to be a fashion designer, and every time Isabel visited, he brought out some of his sketches to get her opinion. Jen knew that Tran hoped Isabel would actually like one of his designs well enough to have it made into an outfit. If she wore it someplace where there were lots of photographers, it would be a big boost for Tran.

That hadn't happened—so far—and Tran sometimes worried that he'd lost his chance for fame and fortune. When he was in a depressed mood, his cooking suffered too. So Jen hoped Isabel's arrival would produce some tasty meals.

"Isabel," Tran said, shaking his finger at her after he finished hugging her, "I read you've retired from modeling."

"Is that true?" asked Mama, her eyes wide with surprise.

Isabel shrugged. "I'm pretty old to be modeling, but I'm still doing a few shoots. Anyway, it got to be boring. And I really don't mind, ever since I heard about the elephants."

"What elephants?"

"*The* elephants. All over. They're endangered, you know. Poachers kill them for their tusks, and their feeding grounds are shrinking. An elephant can eat five hundred pounds of grass a day. Did you know that?"

Mama smiled. "A lot more than a model can," she said.

"Oooh, now you won't care how fat you get. I can fix delicious meals for you," Tran said with a big smile.

"But that's not the point," said Isabel.

"You want to *save* the elephants?" asked Jen.

Isabel beamed at her; to Jen it felt like the sun was shining for her alone. "I'm glad somebody gets the idea," said Isabel.

Both Mama and Tran looked worried. "Isabel, how can you save the elephants?" asked Mama. "Even if they need saving."

"They do, take my word for it," said Isabel. "And what I can do is get publicity for them. Once people learn what's happening, they'll want to stop it."

"I see," said Mama, but Jen could tell she didn't really.

"You ready for gazpacho with shrimp soup?" asked Tran. To him, the solution to everything was to eat. He had told Jen that was because when he escaped from Vietnam he once went two weeks without food.

But Isabel wasn't here for the food. "I was hoping you and Sam would make a contribution," she told Mama.

"Let's eat and we'll talk about it later," said Mama.

Jen knew what Mama was thinking: Daddy wasn't a save-the-elephants kind of guy.

T H R E E

Be Like Mike

DECEMBER 20, 1999

MALCOLM PRETENDED HE DIDN'T HEAR HIS mother calling. He wrapped the pillow over his ears and looked around his room at the posters on the walls. He wished he could be one of the people on them: Michael Jordan, Charles Barkley, Scottie Pippin, Kobe Bryant. Be like Mike.

Or even if he couldn't be like them, at least he wished he could be sixteen. Then he'd go get a job and rent a room of his own. If he wanted, later on he'd get a basketball scholarship to some college. He was a good enough player for that. Or maybe skip college and go right into the NBA, the way Kobe Bryant did.

25

Malcolm

Lying on the bed, Malcolm used the remote control to turn up the volume on his stereo. It was playing Dr. Dre. Malcolm knew that would only irritate his mother more, but at least for a little while it would drown out her voice.

It did, but only for a minute. Then she started banging on his door and he knew he'd better get up. He unlocked the door and saw Mama's angry face.

"Have you got your homework done?" she asked. "You know your grandmother's coming for dinner."

"Yes, Mama," he said.

"It's all done?"

He glanced over his shoulder at the books piled on his desk. He hadn't opened them since he'd come home from school. "Yes, Mama," he said.

"Show me what you've done," she said sharply.

"Um . . . it was all stuff I had to read," he said.

"In math? You had to read something in math?"

"Yeah . . . sort of look over what the book said about quadratic . . . tables and like that." Malcolm knew his mother understood as little about math as he did. She was a lawyer.

She glared at him. "If your father and I get any more notes from your teachers . . ." She didn't finish. The threat was more menacing that way.

"OK, OK," Malcolm said. There was a science test tomorrow, but maybe he'd find some time to study for it in social studies class.

"Straighten yourself up," said Mama. "Look good for your grandmother. Wear something besides those horrible baggy jeans."

"We're not going out, are we?" Malcolm didn't mind putting on preppy clothes as long as none of his friends saw him.

Grandma wasn't so bad anyway, he thought, as he found a pair of slacks in the closet. His mother had bought them for him last year, and the legs were too short. Grandma wouldn't mind. In fact, she wouldn't care if he wore the cool baggy jeans either. Unlike his parents, she never treated him like a little kid.

When he heard the doorbell ring, Malcolm went downstairs. Grandma was old but still looked good. Her gray hair was cut short and she wore a black suit that somehow let you know she wasn't somebody you messed with.

Mama tried to look the same way, Malcolm thought, but it didn't turn out the same. She and Dad were kind of stiff—putting on a show like they wanted to be white or something.

"Look at you!" Grandma said, holding Malcolm by the shoulders at arm's length. She glanced down at his trouser cuffs. "You're growing right out of your clothes!" Malcolm shot a look at Mama, who was frowning.

"He has better clothes than these," said Mama, "but he won't put on anything that looks good. Just those baggy pants . . ."

"Well, you were the same way," said Grandma. Malcolm didn't try to hide his grin.

"I didn't wear clothes that made me look like a hoodlum," Mama said. "And boys in those days didn't wear earrings."

Grandma smiled and gave Malcolm's ear a tweak. "Oh, but you wore what your friends did," she said to Mama. "Bell-bottoms, love beads, and those big Afro haircuts. I remember. I don't think you should condemn anybody for their clothes."

"People do judge you by what they see," said Mama. "You know that. Look at the outfit you're wearing."

"I went to the courthouse today," Grandma said by way of explanation. "Judge Walters is retiring and there was a farewell party for him."

"And you wouldn't have worn a torn T-shirt to that," said Mama.

"Well, no," Grandma replied. "But if I were twelve years old and freezing with my friends, I might."

Mama looked confused, but Malcolm understood. "It's *chillin'*, Grandma," he said. "You chill with your friends."

Grandma winked at him.

They sat down to dinner. Fortunately, Dad had brought home a large roast chicken with all the fixin's, including plenty of mashed potatoes and gravy. He had bought it at a carryout place. Mama had never been very much of a cook. She claimed that being a lawyer was more important. Most of the time, Malcolm ate by himself, fixing his own meals—easy things like cheese sandwiches or hot dogs. The last time Mama had tried to cook a big meal, not even Dad could eat it.

As far as Malcolm was concerned, he would rather not sit down to eat with his parents. That only gave them another opportunity to tell him what a waste he was.

They tried to do that even when Grandma was here, but she managed to cut them off. "I heard from Marcus the other day," she said.

Mama said, "Oh?" politely. Marcus was Grandma's brother and thus Mama's uncle, but Mama wasn't too fond of him. He lived in Los Angeles, and Malcolm only remembered seeing him three or four times, at family reunions.

Uncle Marcus drew comic books, which was kind of cool. But that wasn't the reason Mama didn't like him.

Marcus was sort of a weirdo. He didn't talk much—hardly at all, really. He liked to draw pictures of people instead of talking to them. He could do it really fast, and Mama didn't like the ones he did of her. They made her look a little too angry or something. Mama didn't like being made fun of.

"Marcus is getting an award from the Cartoonists' Guild of America," Grandma was saying. "It's a lifetime achievement award."

"How nice," said Mama.

"You're all invited to attend the ceremony," said Grandma.

"I don't think we can make it," Mama said quickly.

"I haven't even told you when it is yet," said Grandma.

"Well, we're very busy right now at the firm," Mama said. She looked at Dad, who nodded on cue. He seldom disagreed with Mama.

"It's December 29," said Grandma, "in Los Angeles. And we can all stay over for Nell and Rocco's one-hundredth birthday party, to which you are also invited. It's a good time for you to take a few days off. Especially if what they say about this Y2K business is correct."

"If it *is*," said Mama, "I want to be right here in Chicago instead of Los Angeles."

"*I'd* like to go," Malcolm blurted out. He wasn't sure why—probably just to annoy Mama.

Mama shot him a threatening look.

"I would," Malcolm protested. "School lets out on December 22. I'll be on vacation."

"You should be grounded for the whole vacation so you can study," said Mama.

"Oh, let him go if he wants, Sojie." Everybody looked at Dad, startled.

Mama shrugged. "I guess I'm the only one who seems concerned about Malcolm doing well in school," she said.

"Maybe this isn't the right school for him," said Dad.

"It's the best school in Chicago," Mama retorted. "We're paying eleven thousand dollars a year for him to go there."

"You and I didn't go to schools like that," said Dad. "We seem to have turned out all right."

Malcolm could hardly believe it. His parents were *arguing.* And with each other, instead of with him.

Mama spoke in her firmest voice, the one Malcolm had heard her use when she gave speeches. "You and I fought for our children to have the *right* to go to schools like that," she said. Malcolm had heard her bring crowds of people to their feet with that tone of voice. But at home, it just made him want to go upstairs and turn his stereo up loud.

Dad, on the other hand, never raised his voice, so it was a little hard to hear him now. "What's good for some people may not be good for Malcolm."

"I tell you what," Grandma said, interrupting just in time. "If I promise to make sure Malcolm studies every day while we're gone, will that be all right?"

A tense silence followed, with the three adults communicating through eye contact only. Malcolm wished he could get the hang of doing that.

"Oh, all right," Mama said finally. "I guess I can't convince this jury."

Malcolm tried to keep from whooping. He was already trying to remember if the Lakers were playing at home in late December.

FOUR

A Different World

"YOU CAN TAKE YOUR GAME BOY," MOM TOLD CAL. "It won't hurt you to be away from a computer for a few days."

"You don't understand," said Cal. "My kingdom is open to attack if I don't log on at least once a day to reinforce the castle walls and supply the knights and archers."

"Just put up a time-out sign or something," Mom said. "I sometimes think you're a little too wrapped up in that game. It's not the real world, you know."

It's a lot *better* than the real world, thought Cal. It was a place where he could control things. In the real world, he was a ten-year-old kid who had everything decided for him from the time he got up till he went to bed.

He couldn't even go to school by himself because his father was the ninth-richest man in the world. That meant somebody might try to kidnap Cal or hijack the school bus. So a chauffeur in a car with bulletproof glass arrived every morning at 7:45 A.M. Cal had to be up and dressed by then and had to leave his computer at home.

But when the computer was on, Cal was the ruler of a kingdom with 3,469 villagers, 217 knights, and 639 men-at-arms, as well as a palace with so many rooms he hadn't explored them all

Two popular computer games from the late 1990s

yet. He was not only the ruler—he was the protector. His job was to be alert for bands of robbers, sneak thieves, and above all, armies from rival kingdoms.

Cal liked being king. He was good at it too, because his kingdom kept growing. One reason was because he was watchful for any enemy attacks. The sooner you discovered one, the easier it was to repel it.

Cal also learned how to make alliances with the rulers of other kingdoms. He had developed a sense for knowing which of them would be loyal and truthful, and which were more likely to betray him. Almanac was mysterious, though. He had been loyal to Cal so far, but he was the only one to want to talk to him outside The Game.

However, if Cal totally abandoned his kingdom for much longer than a day, even his allies would move in to take the spoils. For it was taken for granted that anyone who neglected his kingdom was fair game. Anyone who failed to take advantage of the opportunity would be a fool.

But nobody else—that is, nobody in Cal's family—understood that. They thought they could just say, "Get in the car, Cal. Your Aunt Isabel is going to take you off to Nana Nell's house for a while." As if he had absolutely nothing better to do.

He knew why, too. He wasn't too wrapped up in The Game to understand.

Anyway, Jen had told him. "Isn't it cool," she had said. "We get to go all the way down to Los Angeles in Isabel's Mustang."

Cal had shrugged. He regularly reached over 150 miles an hour on Need for Speed games. Riding with Isabel, he wouldn't even get to drive.

"Why do we have to visit Nell?" he had asked Jen.

"Well, the real reason is because Isabel thinks the two of us ought to get out more. She said it wasn't healthy to be cooped up here all the time, especially when school is out. Also I told her that Tran wants to be a designer and thinks Nell can get him a job, so Isabel is going to take her some of his drawings."

"Good," said Cal. "Then he can't bug me about the difference between 'persuade' and 'convince.' But I don't *want* to get out more. Why do Mom and Dad want us to go?"

"Well, that's because the *real* real reason we're supposed to be going is to persuade Nell to come up here for Y2K. According to Isabel, you and I are supposed to be all cute and nice to Nell so that when we get ready to come back here, she'll decide to go along and spend her birthday at our house."

"What a dumb idea."

"It's not dumb. I think Isabel was clever to think it up."

"Ha. She just knows that if she told Dad *anything* he could do to get Nell up here, he'd try it."

"I don't care. We'll have a good time. Nell's house is right near the ocean and we can swim."

"Unless Dad learns that a bunch of kidnappers has captured a submarine and plan to grab us on the beach." Cal gave Jen a sly look as if he were going to e-mail Dad that very message.

"Don't even," Jen warned, pointing her finger at her little brother.

But now Cal had another idea. One that not even Jen could object to. He looked at his watch. Only a half hour to go. That meant he had to break one of Dad's rules, but hey. Isabel would get him out of trouble.

Dad had a workroom high up on the top floor of the house. It had one window that faced the Santa Lucia Mountains. Dad had placed his work-table so that his back was turned to the window. He explained that the view was too distracting.

He glanced up with a frown when Cal opened the door. "What's wrong?" he said. Something *had* to be wrong if you were going to disturb Dad up here.

"I need to take one of your laptops," Cal explained. "We're going to Nell's house and I don't think she has a computer."

"She must have a computer. I've sent her four or five."

"But remember when you wanted to e-mail her?" Cal asked. "She said she preferred getting mail the old-fashioned way, and if you had anything important to say you could call her on the phone. She probably hasn't even *tried* to use the computers."

Cal put on his most solemn and honest look. "And you know, Dad," he added, "I need to do some research on the Net for a school project over the vacation."

"Well, you'll want to keep in touch, too," Dad said. "Send your mother an e-mail every day to let her know you're all right."

"Sure, Dad." It really didn't occur to Dad that the telephone was a means of communication. Maybe that was because the telephone company charged for long-distance calls, while e-mail was free.

"Take this one," said Dad. He picked up an IBM Thinkpad that had been sitting open on a table. He hesitated for a moment. "I've been doing some work on this," he said. "But I've downloaded all the files onto my office computer. Just don't lose it, all right, Cal?"

Dad smiled, and Cal realized that was supposed to be a joke. For anybody in their family to lose a computer would be like, well . . . Cal figured he'd be sent to an orphanage at least.

"Thanks, Dad," he said. "I'll send you an e-mail when we get there."

"And do your best to get Nell to come to her senses," Dad replied.

Cal nodded and hurried off. He had to download his game files onto the laptop before it was time to leave. As for Nell, personally he felt that if Dad couldn't persuade her to come up here to escape Y2K, then there was no way Cal and Jen could do it. Besides, if things really did get hairy after January 1, then the fewer people who were here in the shelter, the longer the supplies would last. So if Nell didn't want to come . . . hey, why force her?

That was just something you learned playing The Game.

After they got on the road, Cal had to admit that riding with Aunt Isabel was pretty cool. She knew how to drive stick shift and used it often, especially after they reached the Pacific Coast Highway. In fact, she took the winding curves so fast that even Cal held his breath as they veered close to the guardrail.

With the top down, they could see way out onto the ocean. Gulls flew up the sides of the cliffs and seemed startled to see the blue-green machine speeding past them.

"I told you this would be great," Jen shouted over her shoulder. She sat in the front seat, which

The Pacific Coast Highway in California

was fine with Cal because that meant he could stretch out in the back by himself. He had a Diskman and a stack of CDs to listen to. He brought the Game Boy too, just so Mom wouldn't be suspicious and learn that he'd borrowed Dad's computer. But Game Boys were kid stuff compared to The Game, where you competed online against thousands—maybe millions—of other people. It was too bad, Cal thought, that he didn't have a wireless modem connection so he could play The Game in the car.

Suddenly somebody plucked the Diskman earphones off his head. He looked up and was startled to see it was Isabel, leaning over the front seat. Cal sat up, alarmed. "You're supposed to be driving!" he yelled. Isabel only laughed before turning her attention to the road again.

"It's a glorious day," she said. "You can listen to music anytime."

Cal shook his head. Isabel was cool in some ways—people at school didn't believe she was really his aunt. But just like Mom, she didn't understand why the online world was better than this one.

"OK, so it's a glorious day," said Cal. He looked around. "But everything looks the same as it did five miles back."

"That's because you're not paying attention," said Isabel. "The ocean is a different color here because the sun went behind a cloud. And see those plants on the cliff down there?" She pointed to some shrubs with silvery leaves and clusters of tiny white flowers.

"Yeah."

"You didn't see those a few miles back."

"Is that important?"

"It is. First of all the plants help keep the road from being washed into the ocean. Their roots hold the cliff together. Second, they're guayule shrubs. The ancient Aztecs used to use them to make rubber balls for their ball games. You know what happened to the losers of those games?"

"What?"

"They were killed."

In spite of himself, Cal thought that was way cool.

"Anyway," said Isabel, "there are lots and lots of plants that might be used for medicine or useful things. That's why every plant is important. Every kind of animal."

Cal thought of a magic plant in The Game that you could use to heal soldiers who were wounded. "How about weeds?" he asked.

"There are no such things as weeds," Isabel replied. "Just plants that people don't want. Somebody *else* might find a use for them."

Cal was annoyed. "There are too such things as weeds. The gardeners are always spraying stuff on the lawn to get rid of them."

"Poisons," said Isabel, wrinkling her nose. "Totally unnecessary. Why would anybody want to put poison on their lawn so grass can grow all by itself?"

"So it looks better," said Cal.

"Huh. Then maybe they should just put down cement and paint it green." Isabel pointed to another group of wildflowers growing by the road. "Doesn't that look better than a lawn with millions of blades of grass all cut to the same size?"

Cal shrugged. Secretly, he agreed with Isabel, but didn't want to admit it. "Whatever," he said.

FIVE

Boxes of Memories

DECEMBER 26, 1999

NOBODY ANSWERED THE FRONT DOOR AT NELL'S house, but it was standing open. So Isabel, Jen, and Cal just walked in.

Jen was surprised to see large cardboard boxes piled up on the Spanish tile floor of the front hall. Peeking around a corner she could see even more of them in the front room. Was Nell planning to move somewhere? Maybe she'd taken Daddy's advice after all.

They heard voices coming from the top of the circular staircase that led to the second floor. Jen looked and saw Nell coming down. For somebody

43

who was ninety-nine, she moved pretty well, even though she had to use a cane.

The trouble was, Nell's housekeeper Caridad wanted to *help* her down the stairs. Caridad herself was nearly seventy and was just getting in Nell's way. The two of them kept telling each other, "Watch out!" or "Step down, now," and they were nearly at the bottom before they saw Isabel, Jen, and Cal.

Jen could see the wheels turning inside Nell's head. She was trying to remember their names. Then she pointed a finger in Isabel's direction. "Ah . . . ah . . . you're Lucy's sister. Don't tell me . . ."

Nell

"Isabel," said Isabel.

"Oh, now you didn't have to tell me. I would have gotten it in a minute," said Nell. She smiled at Jen and Cal. "And these are your children? They look just like you."

"No, they're Lucy's kids," said Isabel. "Jennifer and Cal."

"Mama called to tell you we were coming, didn't she?" asked Jen.

"Why, of course she did," said Nell. She turned to Caridad. "How could you have forgotten, Caridad? Hurry up now, they must be hungry. You might have to order something from the grocery."

Silently, Caridad shrugged and gave the guests a look that clearly meant, "Nobody told me anything about you."

"I'm sorry for all this clutter," said Nell, gesturing toward the boxes. "Let's go outside. There's plenty of room to sit down there." She led them to the back of the house and out a sliding glass doorway. They came onto a wooden deck where flowers planted in wine casks were blooming.

From there, Jen could see the ocean. For a second, she almost didn't notice a man sitting in a wheelchair under the shade of the overhanging tile roof.

It was her great-grandpa Rocco. He had a book in his lap but his head was bowed low. "He's asleep," said Nell when she saw Jen looking at him. "He sleeps all day but then he'll wake up and be lively all night. It's from the days when he ran a restaurant in Chicago."

Jen had heard many stories about the restaurant in Chicago, and also knew it had grown into a national chain called Rocco's Famous Italian Restaurants. It was even advertised on television, but the man in the wheelchair didn't look like the Rocco in the commercials.

"He looks different on TV," Jen said.

"That's not him in the commercials," Nell told her. "That's his son, your mother's uncle Tony.

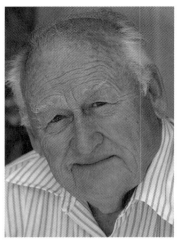

Rocco

Somebody had to play Rocco in the ads, and everybody agreed it should be Tony."

"Are you going to bring Granddad Rocco when you come to live with us?" asked Jen.

"Live with you? I'm not going anywhere. Is your father still bothering about all that funny whitey-kaye business?"

"But all those boxes . . ." said Jen, "I thought you must be getting ready to move."

"Oh, heavens no, dear. It was enough trouble moving out here. I prefer the house in Maine, but Rocco feels much better where the weather is warm."

"So . . ."

"Oh, the boxes? They're filled with things from the house in Maine. I made the mistake of mentioning that I missed something that was stored there. I forget what it was. Maybe my sister's photographs? Anyway, one of my nephews heard me say that, and he took it on himself to start shipping them to me. As a surprise."

Nell smiled, and her blue eyes lit up. "Well, it certainly *was* a surprise. If they keep surprising me this way, I'll have to move someplace else."

"What's in the boxes?" Jen asked.

"Heaven knows. I opened one and found some posters for movies I'd been in during the 1920s. Imagine! I don't think those movies even exist any longer. All that film just disintegrated in the cans."

"Really?" Jen thought old movie posters were cool. "Can I see?"

Caridad reappeared then, bringing a pitcher of iced tea and some cookies. When Jen had a sip of the tea, she was surprised. "What is it?" she asked.

"It's something Caridad invented," said Nell. "It's good, isn't it?"

"What's in it?"

"Oh, she won't tell," Nell said.

"Fresh mint from the garden, ginger, and apple juice," said Caridad.

"She must like you," Nell said to Jen. "She never told me."

"Yes, I did. You just forgot," said Caridad.

It looked like Nell and Caridad were going to argue, but Cal changed the subject. "Does that telephone jack over there work?" He pointed to the wall where Rocco was sitting.

"Why, yes," said Nell. "I had it installed here before we had a cell phone. I still prefer the regular phone."

"So it works?"

"Yes, but there's a telephone inside the house if you want to call your parents."

"No, I want to plug my computer into it."

"Oh, is *that* what you do with computers? No wonder I could never get the hang of using one."

Cal didn't try to explain. He headed for the doorway to get the laptop out of his suitcase.

"He must be just like his father," said Nell. "You know, there has always been a scientist or two in each generation of the Aldriches. My uncle Georgie was the first. He was always tinkering, trying to invent something useful. Probably there are some of his things in those boxes."

"Do you think so?" Jen was interested. "What kinds of things did he invent?"

Nell waved her hand vaguely. "Oh, anything. Probably you could find one of his inventions now and not figure out what it was supposed to be. I don't know what I was thinking about when I said I wanted all that junk. I really ought to throw it out."

"Throw it out?" Jen was horrified. "There might be something valuable in the boxes."

"I suppose," said Nell. "It depends on what you call valuable. It's just old junk to a lot of people, I suspect."

"Oh, no. People collect old things," said Jen. "You could sell them on eBay. You'd get money."

"Oh, it wouldn't be worth the bother," said Nell. "I have enough money. She gave Jen a smile. "And I guess your parents would find a bedroom for me if I ever had to go out begging on the street.

Your father wants me to come and visit so I won't starve."

Jen glanced at Isabel. Nell might appear to have lost her memory, but she certainly knew what was going on around her.

"We can talk about this later, Nell," said Isabel. "But Jen's right. You must have some things in those boxes that you treasure."

Nell looked off into the distance and was silent for a moment. Jen turned her head to see what she was looking at. There was nothing but the ocean.

"Memories," said Nell finally. "That's what's in those boxes." She sighed. "When you have lived as long as I have, you collect a lot of memories. Too many."

She tapped her forehead. "So your mind sorts them out. Maybe rewrites them a little, too. Makes them more pleasant if you're that kind of person. Or if you're unlucky, you hold onto the bad memories instead."

Nell paused to take a sip of the iced tea. "When I've lived through something I don't like," she said, "I don't want to live through it again and again."

She glanced across the patio at Rocco. Cal had returned and plugged in his computer. Jen recognized it. She wondered if Daddy knew Cal had taken it.

"Sometimes," Nell said, lowering her voice, "I think Rocco relives some bad times."

Isabel gave Nell a startled glance. "Grandpop? As far as I can tell, he's done everything he wanted to his whole life. He still treats his sons as if they were about ten, and as for the rest of us . . ." She shook her head and didn't finish.

Nell nodded. "But terrible things happened to him before he came to America, and on the way here. He's been remembering those things lately. That's why he's so quiet."

She pursed her lips. "Maybe there are some things in those boxes that I've forgotten because I wanted to."

They were silent for a moment. Then Nell brightened and looked at Jen. "Do you really want to look through them?" Nell asked.

"Oh, yes," said Jen.

"Well, then I put you in complete charge. And if you find something I won't like, throw it out! Don't even tell me about it."

Jen smiled. "I don't think I'll find anything to throw out."

"Oh, yes," said Nell, nodding. "I want you to."

"Can I start now?" Jen was very eager to see what she'd find.

"Be my guest," said Nell, waving toward the doorway.

Jen didn't wait. She practically ran back to the front room. Now that she took a good look at the boxes, she realized what a big job this was going to be. There were boxes of all kinds and sizes—some heavy cardboard, some wooden crates.

She decided to tackle an easy-looking one first. Taking a pair of scissors from a table, she cut the tape on a brown box that was only as high as her knees.

Pulling open the box flaps, she saw an old camera. When she picked it up, she was a little surprised at how heavy it was. Dusty, too! She wiped her hands on the rug after setting the camera aside.

Underneath it was something more interesting: a photo album. The pebbled-leather black cover was crumbling, and the flakes fell on Jen's clothes as she lifted it.

She opened the album. Old black-and-white photos were pasted inside. She scanned them, turning the pages. A crowd of people . . . police running. Somebody with a sign. Then a boy trying to get away.

A closer picture of the boy. He had a cute smile, Jen thought. Just like . . . who?

It couldn't be him, she thought.

She turned the page. The same boy, better dressed now. He was standing with an old lady in front of a flower bed. And then another picture of him with a girl.

Jen brought the album close to her eyes so she could study the girl's face. It was hard to tell, but yes, it must be Nell. How cute she looked. She and

Rocco were about the same age as Jen was now. Strange to think that they could ever have been that young.

Another page, and this time there were a lot of guests. A party of some kind. Relatives? What sort of party? Maybe Nell would remember. And there was Rocco, dressed up in a suit with knickers and kneesocks. Nell too, wearing a beautiful party dress.

Then a blank page. The rest of the album was filled with people making a movie. Nell, a little older now, was wearing a costume. Jen guessed she was supposed to be a girl in the American Revolutionary times. But no Rocco in these pictures.

Another movie followed, with Nell dressed as a princess. Another one . . . Jen flipped through the pages. Lots of movies. But no Rocco anymore. Rocco was gone.

Jen was disappointed, but she didn't think Nell would want to throw this out. She opened another box, hoping to find more photo albums. Instead, it held some old dresses. She took one out and shook it so that it unfolded. It was silk, a kind of peach color with fringe and very short. Jen held it up to herself, looked in a mirror, and giggled. It was a flapper outfit from the 1920s.

Inside the box was a string of beads that went with the dress. Jen tried them on too. Finally, she found a purse, a very small one, with silver embroidery that made it look very elegant. It had a long silver chain so you could wear it over your shoulder.

Jen hesitated, but then remembered Nell had told her she could look through anything. So she opened the purse. She found a couple of coins, and then looked closely at them. They were real gold coins. One said five dollars on it; the other ten dollars. Nell wouldn't want her to throw *these* out, for sure.

Jen picked something else from the bottom of the purse. It was an old book of matches—dark red with black lettering. Jen's heart fluttered when she read what was printed on it: "ROCCO'S

RESTAURANT, 350 Fullerton Avenue. LIncoln 4545."

Jen recognized the address and knew that LIncoln 4545 was an old-fashioned phone number.

If this purse was Nell's, that meant she had been in Grandpop's restaurant, the very first one. When was that? Had Nell been meeting Grandpop there for some reason?

Jen looked inside the purse again, wondering. She spotted a piece of cheap paper so old and fragile that it nearly split along the creases when she unfolded it. Jen shivered, wondering if it had been a note from Rocco.

But no. It was a drawing. A strange drawing of Nell that made her look like an angel. It was definitely Nell, though.

Very strange, thought Jen. As far as she knew, Rocco never drew pictures. Who could have drawn this one?

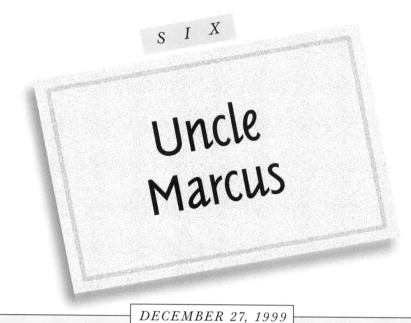

SIX

Uncle Marcus

UNCLE MARCUS LIVED IN A HOUSE WAY UP IN A canyon above Los Angeles. From the outside it reminded Malcolm of a house from . . . well, a cartoon, really. First of all, it was painted a funny color, sort of reddish purple. Then it had rounded-off corners as if somebody had made it from clay that had been smoothed out—even the chimney, which was a bright red.

As they walked toward it, Malcolm saw a plaster face affixed to the front door. It scowled at them. Underneath was a sign that read, "KEEP OUT."

Grandma pointed to the face and told Malcolm, "That's where the doorbell is. Want to ring it?"

Malcolm studied the face and saw that both of its eyes were buttons. He pressed one and jumped back when the face shouted, "Ow!"

He realized in a second that there was a speaker built into the mouth. He tried not to show how embarrassed he was at having Grandma see him jump.

Before Malcolm could say anything, the door opened. There stood a man who was a little shorter than Malcolm. He didn't look very old at all, even

though he must be almost as old as Grandma. He wore jeans and a gray sweatshirt covered with ink stains. In the center of the shirt was a very faded image of the Masked Crusader, Uncle Marcus's most famous comic book character.

He looked surprised to see them. His mouth formed a big O, but no sound came out. Then Grandma stepped forward and gave Uncle Marcus a big hug that pushed him a couple steps backward.

Marcus

Malcolm followed them into the house, listening to Grandma. "You look like you weren't expecting us, Marcus," she said. "I told you we'd be here at noon on the 23rd."

"Forgot," Marcus muttered.

Malcolm looked around. The room was sort of the way a kid's room might look if nobody had told him to clean it up for, say, sixty or seventy years.

Stacks of old comic books were everywhere. Malcolm guessed these must be every issue of *The Masked Crusader*, plus a few thousand more with different characters. All over the walls drawings were tacked up, some only partially finished. It looked like Marcus was working on new characters.

Shelves and cabinets were overflowing with toys and gadgets. Some of them Malcolm recognized—Pokémon figures, Beanie Babies, video games. . . . Others he didn't. There were lots of

Beanie Babies

old tin windup toys that must have been made years ago.

There was a rug in the room, but only a little of it was visible, because it was strewn with pads of drawing paper. Some of them lay open, and Malcolm saw they were filled with sketches of people.

Odd-looking sketches, like the one Uncle Marcus had made of Mama. The people looked partly like animals or machines or cartoon characters. Malcolm saw that the cover of each book had a date and place on it. The one on the top of the stack nearest to him read, "West Covina, 1998." Malcolm cautiously opened the cover and saw what looked like a Chinese girl. Only Marcus had drawn her face as if it were part of a computer monitor, and she had a keyboard built into her stomach.

Grandma introduced them. "This is Sojie's son. You remember your Uncle Marcus. Sojie almost named you after him." Malcolm said hello. Uncle Marcus nodded but didn't say anything. He looked as if he'd rather be somewhere else. Alone.

"Have you got anything to eat?" Grandma asked. "Or should we all go out to lunch?"

Uncle Marcus acted as if this were a tough question, so Grandma just went through a doorway, heading for the kitchen to check for herself.

That left Malcolm alone with Uncle Marcus. There was an uncomfortable silence, and then Marcus reached under a table and came up with a basketball. It wasn't a full-size basketball—more like half-size. Abruptly, he tossed it to Malcolm. He threw it hard so that Malcolm had to bring his hands up quickly to catch it.

He didn't know whether to throw it back or what. But Uncle Marcus waved his hand as if to say, wait a minute. He reached over and flipped a switch on the wall.

Malcolm could hear the hum of a motor, and then saw a backboard with hoop and net come down from the ceiling. Now that was something he'd like to have in his room.

He looked at Marcus, who motioned for him to take a shot. He did. It was harder than it looked. The ball hit the rim and bounced away.

With a cry of glee, Marcus chased down the ball. He turned and in one smooth motion shot it toward the basket.

Swoosh.

Marcus gestured toward the bouncing ball, indicating that it was Malcolm's turn again.

Malcolm picked it up and bounced it to get the feel. How hard could this be? he thought.

He took careful aim this time, but even so, the ball rolled around the hoop and fell off the side.

Marcus was onto it in a flash and, just as easily as before, scored another basket.

When he offered Malcolm a third chance, Malcolm held up his hands. "Hey, man," he said, "it's your court. I can't deal with this little bitty size rock, know what I'm sayin'?"

Uncle Marcus gave a low whistle. The tone of it would have put Malcolm in a fighting mood if it had come from anybody his own age. Marcus turned again, hardly looking this time, and put the ball through the hoop once more.

Grandma appeared in the doorway. "Marcus," she said, "there's nothing in your kitchen except old wrappers from Fatburger. Is that all you ever eat?"

Marcus shook his head, sat down in a chair that was already half full of notebooks, and reached for a drawing pad.

"What happened to that housekeeper I hired for you the last time I was here?" Grandma asked.

Marcus tested a pencil on the paper, didn't like it, and looked for another one in a holder on a table next to the chair.

"Marcus?" asked Grandma again.

"Oooo," he said, sort of letting out breath noisily as if that were a bad memory, "wanted to clean."

"Wanted to clean?" said Grandma. "Who wanted to clean? The housekeeper?"

Marcus nodded. "Buy food OK," he said—so softly that Malcolm wasn't sure he heard right.

"But clean no." Marcus gestured around the room with one hand, while he drew with the other. "Not clean. Not throw out. Not put away. Need," he explained.

"Honestly, Marcus," said Grandma, "I don't know how you've survived all these years without somebody to watch over you."

"You," he murmured, concentrating on the drawing. "Lorraine always watching Marcus." He turned his pad around so she could see it.

Malcolm leaned forward to look. The drawing showed a very big Grandma staring through a pair of huge binoculars at a tiny little creature that you could tell was Marcus the insect.

"All right, all right," said Grandma. "You made your point."

Marcus flipped to the next page of the drawing pad and began work again. Malcolm wondered what was next. Uncle Marcus was funnier than he had first thought.

"I suppose I'm going to have to take you some-place to rent a tuxedo," Grandma told Marcus. "The Cartoonists' Guild banquet is Friday night."

Marcus frowned and shook his head.

"No? Does that mean you already have one?" Grandma asked.

"Not going," Marcus said.

"Not going?" said Grandma. "You have to go. They're giving you an award."

Marcus shrugged. "Don't want."

"But it's an honor. These are all the most important cartoonists in the United States. They're showing you how much they like your work."

Marcus was deeply involved in the drawing now, and didn't respond. But when Malcolm tried to take a peek, Marcus lifted the pad to hide it.

Grandma was mightily annoyed, as she herself liked to say. "Well, I don't know about you, Marcus," she said. "I just don't know. Malcolm and I came all the way out here to see you get this award. All the way from Chicago. And now you just don't feel like showing up."

"Stay here," said Marcus. "Nice visit." He nodded in Malcolm's direction. "Teach him to play basketball."

"Hey," said Malcolm.

"Oh, basketball he knows already," said Grandma, who hadn't seen the game Marcus and Malcolm had played. "His mother made me promise he'd study every day—not play basketball."

Marcus put the finishing touches on his drawing and turned it around so Malcolm could see. It showed Malcolm trying to dunk a tiny basketball that was about the size of a marble. Only Malcolm was several feet short of actually reaching the hoop, and was about to crash into the wall.

"Very funny," said Malcolm. "Now I see why you live alone."

"Malcolm!" scolded his grandmother. "That's a terrible thing to say. Apologize this minute."

But Uncle Marcus thought it was funny. He was laughing—sort of. It was a kind of series of squeaks and cackles. There was no doubt that he was smiling, though.

Finally, Uncle Marcus said, "Right, right. Who would let me have all this fun?" He gestured around, and Malcolm understood. Sure, if somebody else lived here they'd make you clean up your room.

Nell's
Web Site

DECEMBER 27, 1999

CAL WAS PLEASED TO FIND THAT ALL HIS GAME FILES were operating just as well on the laptop as they did on his desktop back home. He should have brought external speakers, but they weren't absolutely necessary.

With the help of Almanac, Cal had taken big chunks of Sir Roger's territory. It was even possible to knock Sir Roger out of the game completely and enslave his citizens.

Cal decided to leave that up to Almanac. There was enough for Cal to do, organizing and redefending his larger domain. That was the trouble with gaining new territory.

A couple of things worried Cal. One was that Almanac might turn against him in some way. He was a clever player and knew how to make alliances effectively.

The other thing that bothered Cal was that Almanac continued to ask for real-world information. It was harmless, Cal thought. How old was he? Cal lied and said he was sixteen but somehow Almanac found out that wasn't true and chewed Cal out. He said if Cal lied to him again, he'd make sure Cal's domain would be destroyed.

But Cal got a good return for telling Almanac silly things like what mountains he lived near, what he could see from his bedroom window, and even telling him what school was like. As if anybody cared about that.

Cal logged on earlier in the day now, when Almanac wasn't around. He probably had a job. Cal didn't know why, but he figured Almanac was grown up. Of course, lots of older people played The Game. Some of them chatted on the community bulletin board, and even made dates. Forget that! If Cal ever met somebody off line they'd probably turn out to be really, really weird.

"Cal, I want you to help me with something." That was Jen. Cal figured once he came down here to Nell's house, nobody would bug him. But noooo.

"I'm not going to help you go through all that junk," he said.

"That's not it. Not exactly, anyway. I had an idea."

"Sleep on it and maybe it will go away."

"Ha, ha. No, look," said Jen. "I found this camera. It's a digital camera. Daddy sent it to Nell, but she never opened it. You could hook it up to this computer, right?"

"Let me see." He examined it. "Yeah, I guess. But what are you going to do with it? You're not really going to put all that junk up for sale on eBay, are you?"

"No, but I thought we could do a Web site for Nell."

"A Web site?" Somehow, Cal didn't connect Nell with Web sites.

"Yes," there are all these old pictures of her and posters from her movies, ads for the TV show—every kind of thing that would look really cool on the Web."

"OK, so go ahead."

"Well," said Jen, a little reluctant, "you see, you're really much better at that kind of stuff than I am, and besides you've got Daddy's computer with the modem all hooked up."

"Yeah, well, I'm also *using* this computer."

"Oh, just for that stupid game. Maybe you

should go down to the beach. Or play basketball. Did you know Nell has a basketball court out back?"

"Yeah, but one, I don't have anybody to play with, and two, I don't like basketball. Other than that it's a great idea. Why don't you go to the beach?"

Cal turned back to the computer game, hoping his sister would go away. Instead, after a second's thought, she said, "You know, I'll bet Mom doesn't know you took Daddy's computer so you could spend all your time playing games. I don't think even Isabel knows you had it in your duffel bag."

"Isabel knows," he muttered. "She can see me using it, can't she?"

"Everybody thinks you're doing homework. Anyway, Mom *doesn't* know, does she?"

Cal frowned and tried to concentrate on the game. But Jen just kept standing there, so finally he said, "All right. Let's make it quick. What exactly do you want me to do?"

Jen didn't hesitate. "Just sort of set up the site and show me how to download pictures onto it from the camera. I may need some more help later."

At least that would make her stop bugging me, thought Cal. "OK, look," he said. "Why don't you take some pictures first?"

"I was hoping you'd help me with that too," she said.

He shook his head. Just then a message appeared on the screen.

> ALMANAC: Hi, Cal. Are we still friends?

Looking over Cal's shoulder, Jen read it. "Oh, who's that?"

"Nobody," said Cal, typing rapidly.

> BLAISE: I can't talk now.
>
> ALMANAC: Busy? You're usually online later than this. And your school vacation must have started, so you should be on a lot now.
>
> BLAISE: Yeah, but somebody's here.

Cal turned the computer so the screen was facing away from Jen.

"Oh, you don't want me to see what you're typing?" said Jen, moving to follow the screen. "Why not? Maybe it's a girl! Has Cal got a *girl* friend?" she chanted.

> ALMANAC: Who is it? Your dad? The software wizard?

Cal was sure he hadn't told Almanac anything about Dad, but there wasn't time to think about that now.

> BLAISE: No, it's just my sister.

"Just your sister?" said Jen, acting hurt.

ALMANAC: Oh, we can't share our secrets with her there. I'll see you later, Cal. Bye.

Almanac logged off The Game. So did Cal. "OK," he said to Jen, "let's find someplace where you can set up a free Web site."

"Wait a minute," said Jen. "Who was that you were talking to?"

"Nobody. Some guy who plays The Game."

"What kinds of secrets do you share with him?"

"Nothing. He's kidding. Look, you want me to do this for you or not?"

"All right," said Jen. "It's really for Nell, you know. Maybe we can set it up by the time her birthday comes."

"First we have to see how much stuff you want to put online. Then we'll know how big a Web site you need."

They went into the front room where Jen had already set aside some of the best things she'd found.

"How many movie posters do you need?" Cal said when he saw a stack of them.

"I just think they're cool," said Jen. "That old-fashioned art and all."

"Look at this," said Cal, picking up a small booklet. "*Trips to the Homes of Movie Stars*," he read from the cover. "Do you think Nell's house is in here?"

"I've looked it up," Jen replied. "It's not only in there, but somebody even checked the address with a pencil. Why do you think that booklet wound up in these boxes?"

"No idea," Cal said.

Another voice came from the doorway. "Let me see that." They turned and saw their great-uncle Tony.

"What are you doing here?" Jen asked.

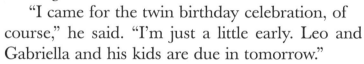

"I came for the twin birthday celebration, of course," he said. "I'm just a little early. Leo and Gabriella and his kids are due in tomorrow."

"I nearly forgot," said Jen. "We're supposed to get Nell and Rocco to come back to our house. Daddy says they won't be safe if they're here when Y2K comes."

Tony laughed. "I don't believe all those warnings. The world's not coming to an end. When midnight comes on December 31, I just want to be celebrating a new millennium—not huddled in some bomb shelter."

He took the movie star guide from Cal and flipped through it. "I think this was the map I used to find my way here when I was a kid. Did I ever tell you how I made my way across the country during the Depression?"

"Yes!" Cal and Jen both said together.

"I might have, I guess," Tony said with a smile. "Nell took me in and showed me what I ought to do with my life."

Nell herself appeared just then, holding her arms out for a hug from Tony. "As I recall," she said, "you snapped me out of a blue funk too. I thought my career was over, but you and David got me going again."

"Who's David?" Cal asked.

A shade of sadness passed over Nell's face. "Don't you even know who David was?" she said. "That's a shame. He was lost in the war. People should remember."

"We want to," said Jen. "You've got to write down the names of all your relatives for us."

"Oh, my goodness," Nell said. "I'd need a week to do that. Why do you want it?"

Jen looked at Cal. "I've . . . I mean, Cal and I are going to make you a surprise on the computer for your birthday."

Nell threw up her hands. "Oh, that will be a surprise," she said. "Is it going to take over my house and turn the lights on and off?"

"We could do that if you wanted," said Cal. "So that when you left a room the light would automatically turn off. Or when you came in, it would turn on. We've got that in our house."

"Yes, but if you try that *here*," said Nell, "I'll send you packing. I like to be the one who decides if I need a light on or not."

"Actually," said Jen, "we thought we'd build you a Web site."

"But if you don't want it—" Cal began, hoping she wouldn't and he could get back to The Game.

Jean realized Nell might not understand, so she said, "A Web site is a place on the Internet that has stuff about you."

"Oh, I know that," said Nell. "When I was in that movie . . . you know, the last one I was in . . ."

"*Dominoes*," said Tony. "You were better than ever."

"That was it," said Nell. "Well, anyway, the studio made a Web site to advertise the picture. They said you could reach young people that way. It must have worked because the movie did very well."

"And you got an Oscar at last," said Jen. "I remember seeing you accept the award on TV. Mom was really excited for you."

"Well, so having a Web site was lucky for me once," said Nell. "Go ahead and set up another one." She paused. "Are you allowed to have two?"

"We could really do it better at home," Jen said. "Why don't you come up and visit us for your birthday?"

Nell shook her finger at Jen. "That isn't going to make me leave," she said. "Everybody I know is invited to come here to celebrate a new millennium, and the two birthdays at the same time. Tell your father I will be quite annoyed if he doesn't come."

Jen nodded. She was pretty sure that Nell couldn't be budged. Now she just hoped Daddy would let her and Cal stay here. The thought of spending New Year's Eve in that underground bunker was just too depressing.

Tickets
for the
Game

DECEMBER 27, 1999

"THE TROUBLE WITH MARCUS," SAID GRANDMA, "IS that even when people were prejudiced against us, he didn't want to fight back."

It seemed to Malcolm that Grandma was driving the car they'd rented a little too fast. She had lost her argument with Uncle Marcus. He still refused to go to accept the cartoonists' award. Malcolm had never figured out why. If somebody were giving *him* an award for being the best basketball player, he'd sure go pick it up.

"What was an S.S. Kress?" Malcolm asked.

"What?" Grandma said.

75

"An S.S. Kress. You told Uncle Marcus that years ago you and Mama had fought for the right to eat at an S.S. Kress lunch counter, and so he ought to accept the cartoonists' award as a tribute to all black people who fought for their rights."

Grandma looked annoyed, as if Malcolm should have learned this somewhere. Probably they did mention it in social studies class. He didn't remember.

"An S.S. Kress was a store where you could buy all sorts of things cheap."

"Well, why'd you want to eat there in the first place? Probably you could have better food at a Mickey D's or Burger King."

"There were no such things in those days. This was in Pickettsville, Georgia, where I was born."

"A restaurant, then. They must have had *some* kind of restaurant."

"Not for black people. Not in that town."

Malcolm shrugged. "So anyway, you moved to Chicago, right?"

"Exactly," said Grandma. "Things were better there, but we found prejudice in Chicago too."

"Didn't stop you from becoming a lawyer."

Grandma slapped the steering wheel, surprising Malcolm. "You think that was easy?" she said. "I had to study at night while I held a job during the day and another one on the weekend. Nobody wanted women or blacks in law school in those days, and I was both."

Malcolm felt uncomfortable. He hated to hear about those days. Grandma thought it was really important for blacks to eat with whites, go to the same schools they did, even swim in the same pools they did. Well, you could do that now, but Malcolm didn't want to.

"Uncle Marcus is probably just shy," said Malcolm, hoping to change the subject.

"Shy?" said Grandma. "Of course he's shy. That's why he's so good at drawing. It was his way of dealing with prejudice."

"Maybe he just likes to draw because he's good at it," Malcolm suggested.

Grandma brushed that thought away with a wave of her hand. "The point is," she said, "all of us had to make sacrifices—so that your generation could have anything it wanted."

Malcolm slumped down in the seat. Next, he knew, would come the message he always heard from Mama. Now that he could be anything he wanted, he had to want what Mama thought was the best thing to be. Lawyer, doctor, scientist—something like that. Not a basketball player, that's for sure.

"We do have what we want," he said.

But Grandma continued as if she hadn't heard. ". . . so even if Marcus is shy—and I know he is—he's got to do this."

"What? Accept an award?"

"Yes, because he is the first black cartoonist to receive the lifetime achievement award from the Cartoonists' Guild. That shows it is yet another field in which our people can excel."

"Well, Uncle Marcus did that anyway, whether he gets the award or not."

"Yes, that's true. But the award is a symbol. It's like the diploma you receive when you graduate from college. Yes, it's just a piece of paper. You're no smarter than if you didn't get it, but it *means* something."

Grandma gave Malcolm a look. He knew what it meant. We expect you to get some of those pieces of paper, Malcolm.

He shrugged. "Well, if Uncle Marcus doesn't want to do it, how can you make him?" Malcolm figured that in most cases, once you were grown up and got to be as old as Uncle Marcus, you probably wouldn't have to do what somebody else wanted, unless you decided to.

But Grandma had different ideas. "We'll drive over and see Nell. I'm invited to her birthday party on the thirty-first, but if we drop in a few days early, she won't mind."

Malcolm had heard about Nell ever since he was very young, but he'd never seen her. Not in person, anyway. He got her mixed up with the characters she had played in old movies.

"Is she still alive?" he asked.

"Hanging in there," said Grandma. "This will be her one hundredth birthday. She's just as old as the century."

Malcolm thought of the spooky old house where Nell had lived in the movie *Shadows of the Oaks*. She hadn't come out ever since a terrible accident had disabled her the night before her wedding. It would be cool if her real house were anything like that.

"But how is she going to help you get Uncle Marcus to accept the award?" he asked.

"Marcus has always idolized Nell," Grandma said. "If she tells him he ought to go, it could make a difference."

Malcolm still didn't understand why it was such a big deal for Marcus to actually go pick up the award. Suppose they made him give a speech? How was *that* going to make blacks look good?

When they reached Nell's house, Malcolm was a little disappointed. It was hidden behind a tall hedge. There weren't any big iron gates or a guard to stop them. Since Grandma knew where it was, she turned right into the driveway.

"I thought she was rich," he said.

"She's rich in friends," said Grandma. "She made a lot of money, but gave plenty of it away to help people. That's the best investment. Anyway, look at her house. It's grand enough, isn't it?"

"Yeah, it's OK," said Malcolm. "Big, but I've seen bigger ones, and it's kinda tacky with that Spanish look. I bet Kobe Bryant's house is bigger."

When they got out of the car, a man standing near the house waved. As he came toward them, Malcolm saw that he was using leg braces to walk.

Grandma gave him a big hug. "Dick," she said, "it's so good to see you again. Have you met my grandson, Malcolm?"

The man offered his hand. Taking it, Malcolm was surprised at how firm his grip was.

"This is Dick Aldrich," Grandma said. "One of Nell's nephews."

"We're sort of cousins, actually," said Dick. "But we feel closer than that. Are you here for the birthday celebrations? Do you have a place to stay? The house is filling up with visitors already."

"Yes," Grandma said, "we're staying at a hotel. But I came early to ask Nell to do me a favor."

"Come around back," said Dick. "Everybody is out on the deck."

Grandma headed in the direction he pointed. Malcolm hung back with Dick, who moved a little more slowly than Grandma. "Where are you from?" asked Dick.

"Chicago," answered Malcolm.

"Guess you're sorry Michael Jordan retired," Dick said with a grin.

"He wasn't going to last much longer," Malcolm said bravely. "But, yeah."

"What do you think of the Lakers' chances?"

"I don't see how anybody can beat them," said Malcolm. "Kobe might even be better than Michael."

Dick shook his head. "Kobe should have gone to college first. He needs the seasoning."

"I don't think so," said Malcolm. "I'll go right into the pros if I get a chance."

Dick gave him a long look. "You think you'll play pro basketball? How tall are you?"

"Five-ten, but I'm still growing."

"You've got a long way to go."

"I'm already taller than Muggsy Bogues, and he plays in the NBA."

Dick chuckled. "Muggsy is not your average player. What's your plan if you don't get into the NBA?"

Malcolm frowned. That was what his father always asked him. "I think you've got to follow your dream," he said stubbornly.

Dick looked away without responding.

"Don't you think that?" asked Malcolm.

Muggsy Bogues (left) and a teammate in December 1999

"Well, I agree that it seems true," said Dick, "but sometimes dreams change as you get older. My father was one of those actors who always played the hero in movies. Big, brave, saved everybody—that sort of thing."

"He was a movie star?" asked Malcolm. "What's his name?"

"He was Richard Aldrich. He's dead now."

Malcolm hadn't heard of him, but tried not to show it. Dick evidently thought his father was famous.

Dick continued, "I wanted to be just like him when I grew up. That was my dream."

Malcolm nodded, and couldn't stop himself from looking at Dick's leg braces. "Then I caught polio," said Dick. "This was before they found a way to prevent it."

He paused. "Hard to hold onto the same dream after that."

They turned the corner to the back of the house, and Malcolm heard Grandma calling him. "Come over here. I want you to meet Nell."

With a wink, Dick waved Malcolm in that direction.

Nell was seated in a big wicker chair, like a queen. She didn't look a hundred years old, Malcolm thought, although she seemed frail, as if she might break a leg if she stood up too quickly.

She held up one hand and Malcolm clasped it gently. "So you are Sojie's son," she said. "How is your mother?"

"Fine," he said, thinking Nell looked exactly the way she did in the movies. He felt almost as if he were some knight coming to give her news.

"And she's not coming to my birthday party?" A little note of disappointment crept into Nell's voice, and Malcolm felt as if he had to apologize.

"She wanted to," he said, looking at Grandma to back him up. "She and Dad have been pretty busy." *That* was OK to say—they were always busy.

"Well, it's all right to miss the party if you're busy," said Nell. "I just wouldn't like it if they stayed home because of this Y2K business."

Some woman sitting near Nell laughed. Malcolm glanced at her. She was good-looking, even though she might have been as old as his mother. Famous too. He knew he should know her name, but couldn't think of it.

"You're not afraid of the Y2K, are you, Malcolm?" Nell asked.

"No," he said. "I'd like to find out if I could survive on my own."

"Exactly right," said Nell. Her voice suddenly sounded firmer. "You know, I'm going to be a hundred years old. Well, just that long ago, very few people had electricity in their homes. Most had no bathrooms. Certainly no televisions, radios, or those horrible computer things." She pointed to a boy who was playing a game on a laptop at the far end of the deck.

"If we need to," Nell went on, "we can use candles again, and make our own fun." Her eyes twinkled, "I'd like to get all my relatives here and tell stories all night long. I've lived through four wars, the Depression, and seen more presidents than I've liked. I have a lot of stories."

"Let me know if you really mean it, because I'll bring a camera and film it." That came from Dick, who had rejoined the group.

"I almost forgot," Dick told Malcolm. "I have a couple of seats to the Lakers game tonight. You want to go?"

Malcolm was caught speechless. He looked at his grandmother, who told Dick, "I think that's a yes."

A New Player

WHEN THE REST OF JEN AND CAL'S VIVANTI relatives arrived from Chicago, they managed to tear Cal away from the laptop. They all took off for a swim at the beach. Jen slipped upstairs and hid until they were gone—not because she didn't like the beach, but because she wanted a chance at the computer by herself.

Cal had gotten the Web page installed and added things to it whenever Jen found something she liked. But all he would let her do was take pictures with the digital camera.

"I want to use the computer too," Jen had said. "You can't hog it all the time."

"If you need a computer, use one of the ones Dad sent Nell," Cal told her. "They haven't even been taken out of the boxes."

"But the Web page program file is on this laptop," Jen pointed out. "It's not yours anyway. It belongs to Daddy, so you have to share it with me."

"You could have brought your own," Cal shot back. "Don't worry about the Web page. I'll put whatever you want on it. If you fooled with it, you'd just mess it up."

Well. Jen couldn't let *that* challenge go, could she? It was probably true that Cal was a tiny bit better with computers than she was. After all, he had no life outside of computers. But she had some of her father's ability too.

Anyway, she knew Cal's password because she had watched him type it in. So that part was easy. Now she just had to find where he'd put the file for the Web page. . . .

Whoops, look at what popped up. This must be the opening screen for the silly game Cal was always playing.

Wasn't *that* cute? As soon as she turned the game on, the captain of the guard asked for orders. She supposed nothing terrible would happen if she didn't give any. She'd just watch for a while and see what happened. Her guards wore pretty blue jackets.

Some other soldiers appeared, dressed in orange. A pop-up screen appeared in a corner of the monitor. It read:

```
ENEMY FORCES
980 foot soldiers
224 archers
62 mounted knights
2 magicians
Do you wish to deploy? y/n
```

Hmmm. Deploy. Jen wondered if Cal would say yes or no. She'd better decide, because the opposing forces were filling up more of the screen now. She hit the Y key.

Now, annoyingly, a new pop-up screen appeared, with the question:

```
How many foot soldiers do you want to deploy?
```

Well, *all* of them, she guessed. Was she supposed to *know* how many? You probably had to type in a code to find out how many you had. But she didn't know it.

Jen hit the ? key instead. The help screen immediately appeared. But as everybody knows, you can't get help from the help screen. It contained a long list of topics, so long that you needed to scroll down to see them all. Unless you knew the name of the exact topic you wanted. Then you could type it in.

Jen typed Deploy. That produced a definition:

> To move military forces into position to defend against an attack, launch an attack, or as support during an ongoing battle. See Defending, Attacking, or Supporting.

Great.

She typed Defending. Meanwhile, shouts of pain and agony started to come from the computer speakers. That, Jen assumed, was the sound of Cal's forces being killed.

Another screen popped into view. It was a communications box. Jen read the message:

> ALMANAC: Cal, you're in danger, and you're not doing anything to protect yourself.

Jen hesitated, and then typed back.

> BLAISE: This isn't Cal. This is his sister.
>
> ALMANAC: Cal is going to be upset when he finds that you've lost his domain.
>
> BLAISE: Tell me about it. How do you get the soldiers to fight back?
>
> ALMANAC: Press Ctl-Alt-F8 and then use arrow keys to move the soldiers around. To deploy your knights, use Ctl-Alt-F10. But it would help you even more if I attacked the invader from the other side.
>
> BLAISE: Would you do that?

ALMANAC: Sure, but I'd need something in return.

Jen didn't understand.

BLAISE: Like what? I can't mess up Cal's system, or he'll kill me.

ALMANAC: Nothing difficult. Just information. For instance, what's your name?

BLAISE: Jen. But I'm not telling you my last name.

ALMANAC: That's all right. Cal told me. Your name is McShane.

BLAISE: He shouldn't have told you.

ALMANAC: What's the harm? You think I'm going to stalk you?

BLAISE: No. Who are you, anyway?

ALMANAC: I'm just a friend of Cal's. Oh, look out now. That line of red knights is going to breach the north wall of your castle.

BLAISE: What should I do?

ALMANAC: Push Alt-F2 to fire a volley of arrows at them.

Jen did as she was told and was delighted to see a line of archers—in blue—appear at the top of the wall and shoot down at the invaders. Now the screams of pain came from her enemies.

She pushed Alt-F2 again and was rewarded with another stream of arrows from the wall. That was so exciting that she did it a third time, even though the enemy soldiers were now running away.

ALMANAC: Be careful. You'll run out of arrows.

Jen hadn't thought of that.

BLAISE: How do you get more arrows?

ALMANAC: Buy them or trade for them. You could borrow some from a friendly ally. Watch the top of the screen now. Some of Princess Penelope's knights are gathering there. I think they're preparing to charge.

BLAISE: That isn't fair.

ALMANAC: If you tell me what you see out the window of your room, I'll drive them off.

BLAISE: The window of my room?

Jen tried to imagine it. Then she remembered.

BLAISE: That's kind of weird. Are you a perv?

ALMANAC: Well, if you're going to insult me, you can defend the castle yourself. Good-bye. I'm leaving.

BLAISE: Wait. Let me think. OK, I see out the window what used to be a tennis court but now it's the roof of a shelter.

ALMANAC: A shelter?

BLAISE: Yeah, like to protect us against Y2K.

ALMANAC: Of course. Your father would be all pre-pared for that, wouldn't he?

BLAISE: Yes. Are you?

ALMANAC: Oh, I'm ready for anything. Be pre-pared is my motto. And now, we'd better tend to business.

Jen saw that the orange knights were riding toward her castle again. But then some knights wearing an odd silvery color suddenly appeared at the right of the screen. Swiftly, they rode into the ranks of the invaders, cutting them down. One by one, the orange warriors turned back or faded out. Jen had to admit that it was pretty impressive, even though this was the sort of game she usually wasn't interested in.

ALMANAC: That should solve your problem for now.

BLAISE: Thank you. Will Cal know that I've been playing the game with his soldiers?

ALMANAC: Not unless I tell him.

BLAISE: You won't, will you?

ALMANAC: Not if you're nice to me.

BLAISE: I was already nice to you.

ALMANAC: Tell me just one more thing?

BLAISE: Maybe.

ALMANAC: What do you see past the shelter? Beyond where your family's property ends?

BLAISE: Nothing. Just a road.

ALMANAC: What's the road's name?

BLAISE: I don't know. It goes into the town.

ALMANAC: What town?

BLAISE: Spanish Pines.

ALMANAC: Thank you, Jen. You're a true friend. I hope we'll meet again.

Jen was going to tell him that wasn't likely, when Almanac abruptly logged off. The violet-red knights that belonged to him faded from the screen.

The only forces left were Jen's—really Cal's. Jen suddenly felt alone. She had a feeling that she'd given away some secret that she shouldn't have. It was a good time for her to leave too. She didn't like this game anymore.

TEN

Another Dream

WHEN GRANDMA HEARD THAT DICK WAS GOING TO take Malcolm to the Lakers game, she had an idea. "My brother Marcus loves basketball," she said.

"I know," Dick replied. "Sometimes we sit together at the games."

"You do? How do you know Marcus?"

"Every so often he stops by Nell's house and draws pictures of her. He's probably her biggest fan."

Grandma nodded. "We met her long ago when we were children. But I didn't know he'd kept in touch with her."

Malcolm smiled to himself. Grandma seemed surprised that there was anything about Uncle Marcus she didn't know. Maybe Marcus had this whole secret life, like the character in his comic book, *The Masked Crusader.*

Lorraine explained to Dick how Marcus wouldn't accept the award from the Cartoonists' Guild. "I thought Nell might be able to talk him into going," Grandma said, "but she says it's Marcus's decision."

Dick nodded. "Nell wouldn't ask Marcus to do anything he didn't want to do."

"I don't know why not," said Grandma. "She's asked me to do a few things I wasn't keen on."

"But she knows you're a strong person," Dick said with a little smile. "She knows you enjoy helping people."

Grandma shook her head. "I've done favors for Marcus, too. And now it's his turn to stand up and get this award. He was the first popular black cartoonist, and the very first to create a black hero for a comic book. When he gets this award, it marks another milestone for black people."

Dick gave her a thoughtful look but said nothing. Malcolm wondered what that meant.

"Anyway," said Grandma, "maybe if you took Marcus to this basketball game you could talk him into accepting the award."

"I only have two tickets," said Dick.

Grandma shot Malcolm a look, and he knew what she was thinking. If Malcolm gave up his ticket . . .

But she didn't have to ask because Dick saw the look too, and said, "I think I can get another ticket. Jack Nicholson's out of town and he has season tickets in the same row. I'll call his secretary."

"You *know* Jack Nicholson?" said Malcolm.

"He's a very nice guy," said Dick. "Too bad he's making a film in England right now. I'd introduce you."

So that was how Dick and Uncle Marcus and Malcolm came to be seated in the front row of the Forum, watching the Lakers play the Portland Trail Blazers. Malcolm had seen the Bulls play in Chicago a few times, but he was never this close to the court.

When the players ran past, Malcolm realized how big they really were. Dick and Marcus looked like children next to some of the players. Shaquille O'Neal stepped right in front of them to in-bound the ball and Malcolm stared at his feet. Malcolm could probably have put both his own feet inside one of Shaq's shoes.

Toward the end of the third quarter, Kobe Bryant dove for a loose ball and crashed into their section of the seats. Malcolm managed to get out of his way in time, but Kobe landed pretty much on top of Dick.

Malcolm and some people in the row behind them helped Kobe get up. Everybody looked at Dick, thinking that he must have been squashed flat.

Kobe reached for Dick's hand and pulled him to his feet as if he were lifting a doll. "Hey, Dick," Malcolm heard him say, "you OK, man?"

Dick looked a little shaken but gave a hardy grin and said, "No prob, Kobe."

Bryant ran off and the others got settled in their seats again. Malcolm couldn't help asking, "You know Kobe Bryant too?"

Kobe Bryant

"I met him at a party at Arnold's house," said Dick. "He's a very nice guy."

After the game, they got back into Dick's limousine and he said, "Let's get something to eat."

"Can we go where the players go to eat?" asked Malcolm.

"Most of them are too tired to go anywhere," said Dick. "You still think you could play ball with them?"

"Maybe," said Malcolm stubbornly. "I'm still growing. I'm only thirteen."

"Yeah, you should be as tall as Shaq if you keep growing till you're, oh, forty-two or forty-three."

Malcolm was annoyed. "Listen," he said, "did my grandma ask you to talk me out of trying to get in the NBA or . . ." He nodded toward the backseat, where Marcus was sitting.

"That's right," said Dick. "I almost forgot." He looked in the rearview mirror. Marcus was examining the contents of a little refrigerator back there.

"Hey, Marcus," said Dick, "are you going to accept the cartoonists' award or not?"

"Not," said Marcus.

"Then that's all settled," Dick said. "Where do you want to go to eat? Spago?"

"Fatburger," came the reply.

Malcolm leaned toward Dick and spoke in a low voice. "Aren't you supposed to talk him into accepting the award?"

"You try," said Dick.

Malcolm turned around and looked into the backseat. Marcus was drinking from a bottle of orange juice. "Uncle Marcus," he said, "why won't you accept the award? I would, if they were giving it to me."

"Why?"

"Well . . . because it shows you're kinda the best."

Marcus shrugged. "If I the best," he said, "don't need award to prove it."

"He's right there," said Dick.

Malcolm ignored him. "Well, Grandma wants you to accept the award," he told Uncle Marcus. "Why not do it for her?"

"She just thinks it's good for black people," said Marcus.

Something was wrong. Malcolm felt frustrated, just the way he had when he played indoor basketball with Uncle Marcus.

"You know," Malcolm said, "you talk better than you did before."

Dick laughed. "Marcus can talk just as well as you or I can," he said.

"Sh, sh, sh," said Marcus, putting his finger to his lips. But Malcolm could see that he was smiling behind the finger.

"You can?" said Malcolm. "Really? Then how come you act like you can't?"

Marcus shrugged, and drank some more orange juice. He played with the electric window switch, running it up and down.

"Uncle Marcus?"

Looking out the window, Marcus began to speak. His voice was high and squeaky like a rusty hinge that needed some grease. "It started when I was little. My sister—your grandmother—talked a lot better than I did. So I decided to let her do the talking for me."

He paused, thinking back almost eighty years. "And then something happened that I thought was just terrific. Pow! Wham! Smash!" He hammered the seat three times with his fist and gave Malcolm a big smile. "Just like in the comic books."

"What was it?"

"My mother saw that I liked to draw. I would draw on anything—walls, old newspapers, flat stones, the ground—with anything I could pick up. Anyway, Mama thought that was my way of talking, so she bought me paper tablets to encourage me. We were poor then, I guess, and even though the tablets only cost a nickel or so, Mama sacrificed so I could have them."

He looked out the window and ran the glass up and down some more. "Nickels and dimes—even pennies—were worth something in those days. But later on when I started to make some money, I paid her back. More than paid her back."

"Yeah," Malcolm said . . . "but you could really talk the whole time?"

"After a while I couldn't," said Uncle Marcus. "I was afraid to. I would talk to myself, make up stories when nobody was around to hear. I invented the Masked Crusader and his sidekick, Lucky, that way. But my talking out loud sounded awful to me, so I was too embarrassed to try it. I just kept on drawing when I needed to tell anybody something."

"That's how you got to be so good," said Dick. "Don't forget that."

Marcus nodded. "Just the same way you got to be so good at making movies. Isn't that right, Dick?"

Dick nodded. "Sure, because I spent all my time learning how to do that."

Marcus turned back to Malcolm. "Anyway," he said, "what you should learn from this story is that it's not a good idea to just work on one thing."

"Wait, wait, wait," said Malcolm. "Just hold on there. That's just what you did." Malcolm pointed at Dick. "And him too. That's why you're a great cartoonist."

"Probably," Malcolm said. "But what if it didn't work out?"

"But it did."

"Sure, but there was a lot of luck involved. Suppose I hadn't gotten a job working at a comic book company. Nat Schwartz, the man who hired me, didn't care if I was black, as long as I could draw. If I hadn't run into him . . . I might be a crazy old guy who lives off his sister. Because I couldn't support myself with a real job. I don't know how to do anything except draw."

"You would have made it anyway, because you were so good," said Malcolm.

Marcus shook his head. "No, there are people who are good who never make it."

"I'm the same way," said Dick. "A lot of people want to make movies, but only a few actually do it."

"Yeah," said Malcolm, "well, what I want to do is play basketball. I don't know if you've noticed, but they're not keeping black guys out of the NBA."

"That's true," said Uncle Marcus, "but what if you're not good enough?"

"Everybody asks me that," said Malcolm.

"It's a good question," said Marcus. "There's not much work for a basketball player who's nearly good enough to play in the NBA."

"I've gotta follow my dream," muttered Malcolm. He was saying that a lot lately.

Dick turned into the Fatburger parking lot. "Eat in or carryout?" he asked Marcus.

"Carryout," said Marcus.

"Yeah, more comfortable eating in the car," said Dick. "We have better drinks too." He drove around to the carryout window. "You like bacon and cheese on your Fatburgers?" he asked Malcolm.

"I guess." Malcolm was staring at the waitress who was taking orders at the carryout window. She was a young black woman with skin that looked like caramel covered with honey. She had the most beautiful face he'd ever seen.

The people in the car ahead of them got their order and moved on. Dick eased his car to the window and when the waitress saw him, her face lit up. "Hi, Dick," she said. Her voice sounded like a musical instrument. Malcolm felt like he was in love.

"Hi, Sharleen," Dick replied. Malcolm was amazed. Dick was talking to this goddess just as if she were a regular person. "Let us have three Fatburgers with everything and three large fries."

"Sure, Dick. Anything to drink?"

"No thanks, Sharleen." As she typed their order into the computer in front of her, Dick asked, "Any luck finding a part yet?"

"You think I'd still be here if I had?"

"Well, your first part might not be a big one. You have to break in any way you can."

"I will, don't worry. Remember me if you hear of anything."

"Will do, Sharleen. If I wasn't shooting documentaries, I'd hire you myself."

"I'd do anything to get a part, Dick."

"Just the burgers and fries is all we want now, Sharleen."

When Sharleen handed Dick the bag with their order, she did it with a smile that made Malcolm's heart ache. If she would only smile at him that way.

As they drove off, Malcolm couldn't help himself. He blurted out, "That's the most beautiful girl I've ever seen."

"Well," said Dick, "you haven't been in Los Angeles that long. Wait till you see some movie stars."

"*She* could be a movie star."

"Maybe. Takes more than just good looks. And anyway she's not even the most beautiful *waitress* in town. See, lots of young women—and good-looking guys too—come out here to break into the movies."

"Following their dreams," said Marcus from the backseat. He'd snagged a few French fries from the bag and was already eating.

"And some of them," Dick continued, "just as talented and beautiful as Sharleen, never become anything but waitresses."

"Some go to college," said Uncle Marcus. Malcolm knew that comment was directed at him.

"I could go to college," said Malcolm. "Michael Jordan went to college. North Carolina."

"He probably studied though," said Marcus.

Malcolm ignored that. He looked back at the restaurant. He could barely see Sharleen's silhouette in the carryout window. He hoped she wouldn't give up her dream.

Watch Out!

"LOOK AT THIS," SAID JEN. SHE HELD UP A BIG GOLD pocket watch on a chain.

"That's the famous watch," said her cousin Suzanne, the folk-rock singer. "Don't show it to anybody."

Suzanne had arrived last night with her husband and new baby—four-month-old Dylan. When she heard Jen was opening the boxes from the house in Maine, she offered to help. In fact, she couldn't be *prevented* from helping, Jen thought. Suzanne told Jen she had spent the best summer of her life at Aldrich House in Maine.

"Why shouldn't I show the watch to any-body?" asked Jen.

"Family legend," said Suzanne. "It brings bad luck if you listen to the song it plays. Let me show you."

Suzanne took the watch and flipped open the case. A tune began to play, as if there were a little music box inside.

"Oh, it sounds nice," said Jen. "That couldn't hurt anybody."

"Maybe not," Suzanne replied, firmly snapping the case shut. "But the last person who used this watch disappeared."

Jen's eyes widened. "Was that Chuck Norman? I know about him. He was my father's best friend."

"And one of Nell's favorite nephews," said Suzanne. "When he disappeared, the hotel in Paris sent his luggage back to her. The watch must have been inside it. Chuck would never have left it behind, unless someone . . . "

"Ah, you found the watch!" Jen and Suzanne turned to see a man in the doorway. Anybody who watched news programs on television would have recognized him—Charles Norman Jr., expert on almost everything.

"Charley," said Suzanne. "I'm surprised to see you here."

"I'm sure I don't know why," he said. "After all, I am Nell's closest living relative. Even though there are half a dozen people she calls her 'nephews,' I'm the only one who actually is."

"As I recall," said Suzanne, "you said on *Meet the Media* that Chuck was probably looking into something he should have kept his nose out of when he disappeared. Afterward, Nell gave a statement to the press that you were a clown and had always been a clown."

"Nell is an old woman," Charley said. "One must make allowances for that. It so happens that I was right."

"What *was* Chuck looking for when he disappeared?" Jen asked.

"As I said," Charley repeated, "something he shouldn't have. Impossible to say precisely what. He had so many will-o'-the-wisps to chase. The Kennedy assassination, the Watergate affair, the Iran-Contra scandal, Whitewater—who knows what else?"

Jen recalled hearing her father and Chuck talk about many of those things. Daddy had lent Chuck money to do his investigations.

"But why shouldn't he look into those things?" asked Jen. "Wasn't he a reporter?"

"Those things are over with," said Charley. "The newspapers have already printed everything you need to know about them."

"On the Internet, it says—"

"Oh, the Internet." Charley sniffed contemptuously. "Anybody can write what they please on the Internet. It takes a seasoned journalist to know what you *should* write about those things."

"Somebody like you," Suzanne said.

"Like me, yes," replied Charley. "I have the experience to know."

"That's why you're an expert on television."

"Quite true," said Charley, apparently unaware of Suzanne's sarcasm. "And that's just why my foolish son Chuck *shouldn't* have been looking into things that were too dangerous to investgate."

"You don't think people should know the truth about them?" asked Suzanne.

"I think," Charley said pompously, "that people should know what is good for the country." He gave Suzanne a stern look. "Don't you?"

In reply, Suzanne turned and walked out the door. Jen jumped up and ran after her. "Oh, wait," Jen said in the hallway. "Can I have the watch back? I have an idea for it."

Suzanne hesitated. "What do you want to do?"

"I'm putting together a Web site for Nell's birthday. I thought it might be cool to use the watch."

"A picture of it? Could you do that?"

"My brother Cal could. He's a real geek."

Suzanne laughed. "Well," she said, "I guess it can't hurt."

"Nell said I could use anything I found in those boxes," said Jen.

"She did? Hmm. Well, maybe she didn't know this watch was in there."

"I could ask her."

"Let's do that."

Nell was actually delighted when she saw the watch. "This reminds me of so many things," she said.

Suzanne handed it to her and Nell cradled it in her hands. "I'm just keeping it for Chuck till he gets back, you know," Nell said.

Jen and Suzanne exchanged glances. Nell noticed. "Oh," she said, "I know he dropped out of sight. But he won't miss my birthday. Wait and see."

Suzanne frowned.

Nell popped open the watch case, and the music again began to play. "It sounds different every time I hear it," she said. She gave Jen and Suzanne a mischievous look. "Should I listen to it all the way through this time?" she asked.

When they didn't answer, she closed the lid. "Better not take a chance," she said. "You never know how long your song will be." She glanced across the terrace, where Rocco, half-asleep, seemed to be watching Cal play with the laptop.

"My song's been pretty long already," Nell said. "And Rocco's too. Don't press your luck, I always say."

Isabel appeared then, wearing clogs and a bathing suit. She'd gone to the beach earlier, but now she looked red and annoyed. The cell phone she was carrying seemed to be the cause of the problem.

"I just heard from Sam," she told Nell. "He's threatening to send Tran down here with a car to bring you and Rocco up to his house."

"Tran?" said Nell. "Isn't that the young man whose costume sketches you showed me?"

"Yes," replied Isabel, "but when Sam sends him to do something, he can be . . . forceful. He's a martial arts expert." Isabel glanced at Jen. "Sam worries that someone may try to harm his family."

Nell smiled. "Well, he won't have to use his martial arts on me. I think I'll call a friend of mine and invite a few professional designers over here. That should distract Mr. Tran, don't you think?"

Isabel laughed. "Maybe it will, but Sam told me that in any case I was supposed to bring Cal and Jen back up there right away. He thinks that as the thirty-first get closer, the roads will be clogged with carloads of people."

"Whatever for?"

"People trying to escape to the countryside."

"There's something the matter with that boy," said Nell. "I used to think he was very smart." Jen smiled to hear her refer to Daddy as a "boy."

"In any case," said Isabel, "I don't want him to accuse me of kidnapping. So Jen, you and Cal better pack up your stuff. I said I'd have you back home by tonight."

"Awww," said Jen. "We won't be able to finish Nell's Web site. And that means we won't be here for the party, either."

Nell broke in. "Oh, we can't let that happen," she said. "I was looking forward to having my own Web site." She turned to Isabel. "Help me up. I'm going inside to call Sam. I need to have a little talk with him."

When Nell left, Jen went to tell Cal the news. She could see that he was chatting with that same strange person online again.

"Is that your little friend?" she asked playfully. She hoped Almanac hadn't told Cal that Jen had entered The Game.

"He's not my friend and he's not little," said Cal. "Princess Penelope is attacking me, and I think Almanac encouraged her. He's threatening to become her ally unless . . ."

"Unless what?" Jen asked.

"Nothing. Forget it," Cal said.

"No, really. Tell me. Is he asking you nosy questions?"

Cal ignored her for a second or two, and then asked, "How would you know that?"

"Ummm . . . no reason. But listen, you'll have to log off soon anyway. Daddy talked to Isabel and told her to bring us back today."

"Today?" Cal shouted, and Jen turned her head to see if anybody noticed. Rocco seemed to be the only one, and he just raised his eyebrows.

"I can't leave my domain unguarded while we drive home," said Cal. "They'll knock me out of The Game."

"Nell is calling Daddy," Jen explained. "Maybe she'll persuade him to let us stay."

"What good is that going to do?" Cal said. "I'll have to do it."

"Do what?"

"Never mind," he said with a snarl. "It's only a stupid game, remember?"

Cal rapidly typed something into the laptop. Jen leaned forward to see what it was.

Roughly, Cal moved to block her view. But she had seen enough to figure out what it was.

It was the code number, she realized. The code someone needed to open the gates to their house.

TWELVE

The Speech

THE BANQUET WOULD REALLY HAVE BEEN interesting if Malcolm hadn't felt like he was going to throw up. Cartoonists apparently liked to eat and tell jokes. The waiters offered the banquet guests a choice of burritos, tacos, lasagna, Italian or Polish sausages, and Chinese lemon chicken with fried dumplings.

At all the tables, people were telling jokes, laughing loudly, and drawing right on the tablecloths. As far as Malcolm could see, if you weren't weird you couldn't be a cartoonist.

Grandma just laughed when she saw the menu. "This is not your ordinary rubber-chicken banquet," she said. "I think I'll drop dead with a heart attack if I eat any of this."

Despite the food, Grandma was happy because Malcolm and Dick had talked Uncle Marcus into accepting the award. Or so she thought. She didn't know about the plan.

That only made Malcolm more nervous, because he didn't think he could be funny at all—not in front of a group of cartoonists. And in a few minutes, *he* was going to give Uncle Marcus's acceptance speech.

Two nights earlier, after Dick and Malcolm and Uncle Marcus had finished their Fatburgers, they went back to Uncle Marcus's house. He had lots more toys, games, and fun things to play with. Uncle Marcus and Dick played air hockey while Malcolm read back issues of *The Masked Crusader*. (Actually, both Marcus and Dick were better at air hockey than he was.)

Later they sat drinking soft drinks, eating caramel popcorn, and watching videotapes of *The Simpsons*. Malcolm asked his uncle how he got the idea for the Masked Crusader in the first place.

Marcus smiled. "People always ask me," he said. "But I never tell."

Malcolm was interested. "Why not?"

"Because it's a secret."

"Aw, you can tell me," said Malcolm.

The Simpsons

Marcus gave him a funny look. "Maybe," he said, "if you do me a favor."

"Sure, what?" Malcolm couldn't think of anything Uncle Marcus might want.

"I've been thinking about what Lorraine said. I mean, about the award. She'll be mad at me if I don't accept it."

"Yeah, probably. But I'm sure she'll forgive you."

"I'd like to go," said Marcus. "But I don't want to speak. Suppose you take the award."

"Take it?" asked Malcolm. "What do you mean? Take it where?"

"You know . . . walk up and get it when they call my name."

"Accept it for you?" Malcolm got the idea, but didn't like it. "No, they wouldn't let me."

Marcus insisted. Malcolm looked to Dick for support, but Dick said, "Sounds like a plan. We'll write a speech. All you have to do is read it."

Malcolm's stomach churned as he thought of the times he had to stand up and read aloud in class. "But they're not honoring *me*," he said.

"You'll say you're accepting on behalf of your Uncle Marcus," Dick said. "Everybody knows he's not much of a talker."

"Yeah?" said Malcolm. "Then think how surprised they'll be when they found out he *is*."

By now, the person who was going to present the award was standing at the podium. Malcolm wondered what you did if you had to get sick while you were up there on the stage. His stomach churned. In fact, maybe he should go to the bathroom, just in case . . .

. . . but as he started to get up, somebody put a hand on his arm. It was Dick. "Not yet," he said. "Wait until the introduction is over."

* * *

"The Masked Crusader," Uncle Marcus had told Malcolm, "was my father."

"Your father?" Malcolm stared. He couldn't have been more surprised.

"Yes, your great-grand-father, John Henry Dixon."

"But . . . what . . ." Malcolm struggled for words. "He never wore a cape and ran around saving people." *Did he?* Malcolm was almost *sure* he didn't.

"Well, no," Uncle Marcus admitted. "He was a worker in an automobile factory. Made good money for that time. But before that, when I was very little, he had to escape from the police."

"Wow. What did he do?"

"Basically he stood up for his rights. Only in those days in the South a black man *had* no rights. So he decided to take his family North. But they wouldn't let him."

"Who wouldn't?"

"The white people who ran the town. Didn't your grandmother ever tell you about this?"

"Uh, yeah, maybe. Only I wasn't paying much attention."

"I guess you were shooting baskets or some-thing more important. Well, anyway, the white people knew John Henry Dixon was a good worker. They wanted his work, his body, but they didn't want him to be a real person, a man. So the police would stop him—and every other black man—from getting on the train to leave town."

"So how'd he get away?"

"I'm not real sure. That's when he became the Masked Crusader, in my mind. I knew he'd left us. And I guess that made me afraid. So I imag-ined him as the Masked Crusader, hiding from the police."

"Well, you found him again, didn't you?"

Marcus nodded. "Yes, I'll never forget the train ride. Mama, my two sisters, and I took the train to Chicago. I think it took three days. But Papa wasn't with us. He got there some other way."

"So how come you didn't show he was black in the comic books?"

"Well, he had to disguise himself. And of course, in order to get into a comic book, he had to solve crimes too. I couldn't tell people the *real* reason why he wore a mask."

Marcus pointed to one of the drawings on the wall. "That was what the Crusader originally looked like. But then I started to get letters from people who thought they knew why he wore a mask." Uncle Marcus chuckled. "There were lots of reasons that they'd made up. I remember getting a letter from a Chinese boy. He was sure the Crusader wore a mask to hide his Chinese eyes. The boy wanted me to put a secret symbol in one of the cartoons to let him know he guessed right."

"Did you?" Malcolm asked.

"Oh, sure," said Uncle Marcus. "Why not? He wanted to have a superhero, too."

"But you said that the Crusader was really your *father*."

"Sure," Marcus said, "but he could be somebody else too."

When Malcolm heard the words, ". . . and so tonight the Guild is proud to honor . . ." he sat up and took a deep breath. For about the twentieth time, he reached inside the jacket of the tuxedo Dick had rented for him. The speech was still there.

". . . Marcus Dixon, for a lifetime of high achievement in our profession." The audience applauded and Malcolm stood up, feeling shaky. Grandma gave him a look of alarm. They hadn't told her before, but now Marcus whispered something in her ear. She shook her head as if she disapproved of what she heard.

But it was too late now. Malcolm was on his way to the stage. "There are steps when you get up there," Dick had said, and Malcolm kept repeating to himself don't trip don't trip don't trip.

He didn't. But when he reached the podium and turned to face the audience, he almost wished he had. All those faces . . . watching him.

He opened his mouth, but for a few seconds wasn't able to speak. When he did, he didn't like the way his voice sounded, but he plowed ahead anyway.

"My name is Malcolm Barry. I'm accepting this award on behalf of my great-uncle Marcus Dixon. He said you'd all understand."

The audience laughed in a friendly way, which relaxed Malcolm a bit.

He took the speech out and unfolded it. He started to explain. "I asked my Uncle Marcus how he thought of the Masked Crusader and what made him into a cartoonist in the first place. I wrote out the answers to tell you. But I have something else to say first."

He paused to work up his courage. Maybe this wasn't a good idea, like the time he broke both his ankles because he took a dare to hang from the third-floor window of his school.

"See," said Malcolm, "I learned something about my family from talking to my uncle. And from my grandmother too." He looked out to find her in the audience. "What I learned was where I came from, how I got here. I'm glad I did, because it made me think a little more about where I'm going." He cleared his throat. "Where I want to go."

He spread out the sheets of paper and began to read: "You may not know it, but the Masked Crusader had a secret message. . . ."

THIRTEEN

Schemes

JEN COULD HARDLY BELIEVE IT WHEN SHE SAW HER parents arrive at Nell's house. Nell had shown herself to be more stubborn than Daddy. She had cheated a little, but hey, when you're almost a hundred years old you use every trick you can get.

First of all, Nell made a bargain with Daddy. If even the slightest thing went wrong at midnight, December 31, she agreed to get right into one of the limousines that Daddy would have waiting in front of the house.

Daddy certainly thought he had the better of that bargain. He believed that a lot of things would go wrong, and he had hired professional drivers with fast cars who could make it back to his house in two hours.

Just in case something did happen, Nell was prepared. As soon as she'd gotten off the phone with Daddy, she called a private nursing service. Rocco woke up from his afternoon nap, surprised to find that he now had a full-time nurse standing by him. Or really sitting by, since all she did was read magazines, watch television, and get a pill for Rocco to take three times a day.

"Did Rocco suddenly take a turn for the worse?" Aunt Isabel asked Nell.

"No, he's fine," said Nell.

"So, why . . ." Aunt Isabel gestured toward the nurse.

"Oh." Nell nodded, a twinkle in her eye. "Promise not to tell?"

"I can keep a secret," said Isabel.

Nell glanced at Jen, who was listening while trying not to be obvious about it. "You too," Nell said.

"I'll never tell," promised Jen.

"You'd better not," Nell said. "Because even if the milk curdles, dogs howl, or the moon turns red at midnight on the thirty-first, I still would rather stay here than go to your house, where everybody is safe and nothing happens."

"But you promised Daddy."

"So I did," Nell said. "But if something awful does happen at midnight, it's likely to have a terrible effect on Rocco. The nurse will tell us he had a medical emergency, a doctor will come—and it will be impossible to move him without endangering his health. I, of course, will have to stay here with him."

"Aunt Nell!" Jen was a little shocked at first. Then Aunt Isabel laughed, and Jen couldn't help herself from joining in.

Wiping her eyes, Isabel said, "I thought I recognized that nurse. She's really an actress, isn't she?"

Nell wagged her finger. "Remember your promise," she said. "I thought it would be unfair to use a real nurse, who might be needed by someone else. Besides, the right actress always looks better than the real thing. A director told me that once, and he was right."

Jen thought it was so funny that for a while she stopped worrying about Cal.

She tried to distract him from The Game by thinking up new stuff to put on the Web site. Even so, Cal seemed obsessed by the game now. He didn't like it when Jen sat nearby, trying to get a glimpse of his online conversations.

"I thought you were supposed to be unpacking boxes," he said.

"I've got a lot of new stuff that I need you to download," she replied. "That watch, for instance. Do you think we could have the watch ticking away in a corner of the screen, keeping real time?"

Cal shook his head. "No, you couldn't do that. You couldn't get the hands to move."

"Why not?"

"You just couldn't."

"You're only being lazy," said Jen. "If you weren't talking to that Almanac all the time . . ."

"I'm not," he said.

She hesitated, wondering if she should say this. "Listen, I know you gave him the code to open the gate at our house."

"He doesn't know where the house is, so what's the problem?"

Jen tried to remember the conversation she had with Almanac. "He might figure out where the house is," she suggested.

"No way," snapped Cal. "Anyway, we could get Tran to change the code at the front gate."

Yes, thought Jen. That was something they ought to do.

When Mom and Daddy arrived, it seemed like everybody wanted to talk to them. Jen knew Tran must have driven their car, but in all the excitement she couldn't find him.

One good thing was that Cal couldn't glue himself to the computer after Mom and Daddy arrived. Mom would be annoyed to find out he'd done nothing at Nell's house but play games.

So Jen snatched the laptop when he wasn't looking. Pulling the modem wire out of the wall, she slipped away and ran toward the garage in back of the house.

She didn't have a plan, really. Not until she bumped into Tran, who was unloading the luggage from the car. He gave her a quick look, and she realized he knew something was wrong.

"You going somewhere with that computer?" he asked. "Looks like one of your Dad's best."

"It is. Oh, Tran, listen, I've got to tell somebody. But you have to promise . . ." She hesitated.

"Yes?" he said. "Trouble sometimes becomes obvious, the more you try to hide it."

"I'm afraid," she said. "I think Cal did something stupid." She swallowed hard. She had to tell him the truth. "But it's partly my fault too."

"Don't worry if the only problem is a computer crash," he said. "The files can be recovered."

"No, it's worse than that." Jen began to blurt out the story. She told Tran about The Game, Almanac, and what she and Cal had told him.

When she finished, Tran set down the luggage and folded his arms. He said, "This has all been very unwise. I didn't think you were such foolish children, even though you *have* gone to American schools."

"I'm so sorry, Tran."

"You think this Almanac could find the house from what you told him?"

"I don't know. He seems awfully clever."

Tran picked up the suitcases again. "Let's go inside. People who are clever make mistakes of overconfidence."

After Tran put the luggage in Jen's parents' bedroom, he said, "Where can we find a phone jack?"

"There's one in practically every room," said Jen.

"Then let's go where we won't be disturbed."

Jen felt a little scared when she realized what Tran intended to do. They set up the laptop in a room nobody was using. "Start it up now," Tran told Jen. "I will test my skill at this game."

She did as he asked. When she reached the opening screen of The Game, she could see Cal was in a lot of trouble. His domain was bigger than ever, but it was completely surrounded by another territory—all one color, the color of Almanac's forces.

Jen didn't have to wait long for Almanac to appear in person.

ALMANAC: So, Cal. I thought you left The Game for today. Did you come back to thank me?

Tran nudged Jen. "Ask him why you should thank him."

> BLAISE: What am I supposed to thank you for?
>
> ALMANAC: Why, for defeating your enemy Princess Penelope, of course. Remember, I could have become her ally instead of yours. She and I could quite easily have conquered your domain and divided it between us.

Jen looked at Tran for advice. "But now you've surrounded me," he whispered. Jen typed the message.

> ALMANAC: Yes, that is true. But you have nothing to fear because you and I are friends, aren't we? Otherwise, I could overrun your territory. My forces outnumber yours, I have superior position, and if I'm not wrong, you still haven't found the spell to wake up your magician.

"What now?" Jen asked.

"Tell him you may have figured out the spell," Tran replied.

Why are we whispering? Jen thought. But she typed,

> BLAISE: Don't be too sure I don't have the spell.
>
> ALMANAC: Oh? You're planning a surprise? I think not, Cal. There were several situations lately where you could have used your magician, but didn't. I'll tell you something else. I found a parchment scroll under the floor of the shepherd's cottage. You know what was on it?

> BLAISE: What?
>
> ALMANAC: A spell that I suspect is the one you've been looking for. Now, as your friend, I'm willing to share that information with you.

"Tell him you'd like that," said Tran. Jen did.

> ALMANAC: But first I want to make sure we're still friends. I don't like treachery. I punish traitors severely.
>
> BLAISE: I'm not a traitor.
>
> ALMANAC: But are you my friend? Really a true friend? You know what true friends do, Cal?
>
> BLAISE: What?
>
> ALMANAC: They visit each other.

Jen looked at Tran, who nodded and said, "Don't show yourself to be eager, but let him know he can visit you."

"But he's so creepy," said Jen.

"Don't worry," said Tran. "Tell him to come to the house tomorrow night when your parents are not at home."

"But I won't be there either," said Jen.

"No," said Tran. "But I will."

Finale

NELL'S HOUSE HAD SEEMED BIG WHEN JEN FIRST arrived, but now it was crowded with people. The night before, some of the relatives staying there had to sleep on couches, and the kids in sleeping bags. Suzanne offered to take the overflow visitors to her house, which wasn't far. Jen wanted desperately to go, especially after Suzanne said that Justin Timberlake lived just down the street from her.

But Mom said no. Can you imagine? Mom thought that Suzanne had drug parties or something. "She's not that kind of rock star," Jen told Mom. "And anyway, we're related to her."

"Very distantly," said Mom.

Justin Timberlake of 'N Sync

Some of the kids in the Vivanti family went with Suzanne, and even Uncle Mike, who was a *priest.* Mom was just living in the past, back in the '80s when everybody was taking drugs.

Jen looked at her watch. Six o'clock now. Only six more hours till midnight. Probably nobody would ever go to bed tonight. Either they'd all be heading back to Spanish Pines in the limos Daddy had waiting in the driveway, or they'd be celebrating the new millennium here at Nell's.

Nell seemed pretty sure they'd be here all night. After Jen said she'd found enough things for the Web site, Nell had all the boxes cleared away. She hired some people to decorate the rooms with flowers, balloons, and Mexican paper cutout banners. Christmas lights were strung across the terrace and along the tops of the second-floor balconies overlooking the main room inside.

There wasn't any table big enough for everybody to sit down to dinner. So Nell hired waiters to carry around trays of food from the kitchen. The kitchen itself turned into a battleground. Caridad fixed Cuban and Mexican specialties like *vaca frita*, quesadillas, and tacos. She figured the kitchen was all hers, but other people decided to invade.

Several Vivanti family members came to make what they claimed were Rocco's original recipes. But they started arguing among themselves about whose recipes were the

Part of a Mexican paper cutout banner

genuine originals. Finally Rocco himself had to be wheeled into the kitchen, where he scowled and shook his head at every bite he tasted.

Then Rocco's daughter Gabriella arrived with her friend Silvia. Gabriella declared that only she knew the recipes and Rocco had forgotten them long ago. That enraged Rocco so much that he wheeled himself out of the kitchen, found Nell, and somehow told her that she must throw Gabriella out of the house.

While that was going on, Suzanne and Aunt Isabel, who were both vegetarians, didn't want to eat anything that Caridad or the Vivantis were cooking. So they made a quick trip to a local supermarket and returned with enough vegetables, as their cousin Eric remarked, "to feed a petting zoo."

Since the kitchen was full of squabbling cooks, Suzanne and Isabel sat on the patio and cut the raw veggies into creative shapes—hearts, stars, curls, and whatever else they could think of. Then they sprinkled them with spices and marinades. Actually, Jen had to admit they were pretty good, for vegetables.

The kitchen got even more crowded after Nell's old friend Lorraine arrived with her brother Marcus and grandson Malcolm. When Lorraine saw everybody cooking she said it made her homesick. Not for Chicago, which had been her home for over seventy years, but for Pickettsville, Georgia, the little town where she had grown up. And that meant she had to have chitlins and chicken fried in lard, which horrified Suzanne and Isabel. Even so, Lorraine set out with her own shopping list.

So, Jen figured, whatever other disasters might happen because of Y2K, the people at this party were certainly not going to starve to death.

It was seven o'clock when Tran showed up. Jen was the first to see him, and he shot her a stern look from across the room. It sent a shiver down her spine. She hoped she and Cal wouldn't be grounded for life.

Tran didn't say anything to her, however. He looked around and when he spotted Daddy, went to talk to him. After a few whispered words, the two of them went outside.

Jen looked for Cal, thinking that she should warn him. As usual he was on the terrace with his computer. Rocco was there too, sulking because Nell refused to throw his daughter out of the house. "Listen," Jen said to Cal, "I want to tell you something important."

"The Web site's finished, OK?" said Cal. "I got the hands on the watch to keep time. I even added something you didn't think of."

"What?"

"I made it so people can write in their own messages. Whatever they want to say about Nell. Some of these people have known her for years, right? I mean, all that stuff you collected is good to look at, but who knows what it all means?"

Jen had to admit this was a cool idea. Then she remembered: "I have to tell you about Almanac first."

"Him? Forget him. You know what? He left his domain completely unguarded and the other players just conquered it all."

"Did you take any?"

Cal shrugged. "Nah. You never know, he might come back."

"Cal? Jen?"

They turned to see Daddy standing in the doorway to the house. Oh-oh, thought Jen. Here it comes.

"The computer's fine, Dad," Cal said.

Daddy shook his head. "That's not what I want to talk to you about. Tran just arrived. He had gone back to our house and found that someone had breached the security gates. This person was wandering through the house. It's just very fortunate none of us was home."

"Uh, yeah," said Jen. "Good thing you and Mom decided to come to Nell's party."

"What happened?" asked Cal. "Did Tran shoot the guy?"

"Of course not," said Daddy. "He subdued him and called the police."

"Cool," said Cal, giving his version of a karate kick. "I wish I'd seen Tran take this guy."

"Well, I'm glad you didn't," said Daddy. "Anyway, I've decided that we'll stay here for at least another day. I'm sorry, but we won't be going home at midnight."

Jen and Cal tried to act disappointed, but didn't do a very good job of it.

"What about Y2K?" asked Jen.

Daddy looked uncomfortable. "Well," he said, "we're still prepared for that. Better to be prepared for something that doesn't happen than not prepared for something that does."

Jen and Cal looked at each other. Daddy often said confusing things, but what did he meant by *that?*

They soon found out. Inside the house, television sets were on and the guests were watching New Year's celebrations from various parts of the world. The first place to see the year 2000 had been an island in the Pacific on the other side of the International Date Line. Hour after hour, the new millennium spread westward across the planet. By now, it was January 1 in most of Europe.

And the Y2K disaster hadn't happened. The lights stayed on, TV and radio stations were still broadcasting, water kept coming out of faucets, and people celebrated. Daddy must be embarrassed, thought Jen.

She finally found Tran. He was sitting next to Nell, Marcus, and a couple of other people. Jen went a little closer and saw that they were handing around the costume sketches Tran had made. It seemed as if they liked his work. Tran looked up for a second and winked at Jen.

No need to worry about him.

Nine o'clock came and everybody stopped talking for a couple of minutes to watch the big ball in Times Square in New York City come down. The lights on top of the pole lit up, spelling out 2000. People in the streets celebrated, and life went on. No Y2K bugs.

New Year's Eve celebration in Times Square, 2000

Nell had a television set close to her chair. "I always watch the scene in Times Square," she said, "hoping that I'll see somebody in the crowd who got lost."

"Lost?" said Jen. "You mean lost from their parents?"

"She means someone like Chuck," said Charley Norman.

"Oh, no, not Chuck," said Nell. "Chuck wouldn't be in Times Square tonight. He's coming here." Charley rolled his eyes.

"No," Nell went on. "I mean people I've lost track of. I wonder what became of Sam's parents, my cousin Esther and Ed McShane. Esther was such a brilliant young woman."

Jen looked around. She knew what happened to Esther, who was her grandmother. Daddy didn't want her to tell anyone, but Nell was different.

"We visited Grandma Esther two years ago," Jen said quietly.

Nell gave her a look. "You did?"

"Yes, she lives out in the desert in Nevada with some other people. They build houses out of mud and sticks and stuff."

"There's no need for her to live there," Nell said. "Your father could buy her a nice place. I should have a little talk with him."

"Oh, no," said Jen. "Please don't. Grandma sort of had a fight with Daddy when he suggested the same thing. She said she'd never take any money from him . . . because he makes bad things."

Nell frowned. "What bad things?"

"Computer software. The people she lives with are into a kind of natural way of life, you know."

"I thought she'd gotten over that." Nell sighed. "Well, everybody lives the way they want, I guess. What about your grandfather McShane? Is he living with her?"

"No. Daddy hired detectives to find him, but nobody knows where he is."

"Watch for him in Times Square," Nell said, pointing at the TV.

Jen glanced at Nell nervously. She decided now would be a good time to display the Web site.

Heading back to the terrace for the laptop, she found to her surprise that Rocco had picked it up and was typing on it. "Grandpop!" she said. "What are you doing?" For a second she worried that he was chatting with Almanac, but then remembered that Almanac must be in jail.

Cal appeared then, carrying a tray of clams with bacon. "Hey!" he said when he saw Rocco with the laptop, "You're not—I mean, be careful."

Cal looked at Jen and explained, "Grandpop pointed to his mouth like he was hungry, so I went to get him some food. Gabriella said these were his favorites. I didn't know he'd try to use the laptop."

An IBM Thinkpad

Jen had been reading what was on the screen. "He wanted to be the first one to leave a message on Nell's Web site," she said.

"He did? How'd he learn to do that?"

"From watching you, I guess," said Jen. "Come on, let's wheel him inside. We're going to give Nell her present a little early."

Just as they entered the main room, there was another burst of cheers. It was now ten o'clock on the West Coast, and that meant it was midnight in Chicago. On the television sets, bringing in the New Year from the band shell in Grant Park in Chicago, was a group everybody in Nell's house knew—the Whatevers.

"They're playing 'LUV,'" Jen said. "That's a real oldie."

"Mama's favorite song," said Suzanne, who was the daughter of the lead singer. "She looks good. Nobody would think the Whatevers are nearly sixty."

"Bite your tongue," called Nell. "Sixty isn't the least bit old."

Since nearly everybody had gathered in one room by now, Jen made her announcement when the song was over. "Could I get your attention just for a minute?" she said. "We have a present for Nell, and you can all contribute to it."

Cal held up the laptop so everybody could see. "It's Nell's own Web site," he said, "with a lot of stuff on it that Jen found. But see . . . if you press on this icon, you'll get to an album page where you can write a message."

Everybody crowded forward to see, but Jen called out, "Wait, there's one more thing. Rocco already wrote his message."

That caused some murmuring. Jen could tell what the other guests were thinking. "He really did," she said. "All by himself when we weren't looking."

"What did he write?" asked Leo, one of Rocco's sons.

"It's for me," Nell said, in the voice she used when she played Empress Catherine the Great. Obediently, Cal brought her the laptop.

"Where's Rocco's message?" asked Nell.

Cal hit a key to bring it up, and the screen turned blue.

"Oh-oh," he said. "Screen freeze. Got to reboot."

"Is it running on McByte software?" asked Jen's Uncle Art, the one Daddy called a hippie, even though he was director of marketing for the Rocco's Famous chain. Some good-natured sarcastic comments could be heard around the room while Cal rebooted. "Computers are the reason why everybody works till nine o'clock now when they used to quit at five," said Art.

Finally Cal brought Rocco's message up on the screen. Nell put her reading glasses on and scanned it. Jen thought she saw a tear in her eye. "That's very nice," Nell said, reaching to take Rocco's hand. "Jen, why don't you read it aloud?"

Jen took a deep breath. How did she get into this? But nobody could refuse Nell, so she read:

Long ago, when I left Italy, we had to leave my two sisters behind, for they had been buried in the churchyard. My mother said that we must bring them with us in our hearts. Then my mother died on the ship and they put her into the sea. So I carried her in my heart too. In this country, I could not find my father, and I was all alone. Two angels appeared from nowhere and took me to live with them. I didn't stay long, but I kept them in my heart always. Now my wife Teresita has gone to heaven, and she also lives in my heart. At the end of my life I have returned to be with one of those angels. Her name is Nell. One day soon we will be in heaven and meet all the people I have carried in my heart for so long. Thank you, Nell, for helping make my heart lighter.

When she finished, everybody was silent for a few seconds. Then Rocco's son Leo said, "Pop wrote that, all right."

"Who's next?" said Nell. Charley snatched the laptop from Jen and said, "I am."

For the next hour, everybody took turns, passing the laptop around and typing in their messages. Sometimes the pictures that Jen had scanned into the computer brought back memories of some event in the past. Several of the guests told Jen what a great idea this was.

Eleven o'clock came, and the television now showed the celebrations in Denver. Cal suddenly realized that he hadn't checked on his domain in over an hour. But just at that moment, the person using the laptop to write a message for Nell was Daddy. He didn't understand why it was so important for Cal to use the computer right away.

Tran left the group around Nell and took Cal by the arm. "Come with me," he said. "Let us have a talk about correct behavior." Cal shot Jen an accusing look as they left the room, but she knew that Tran wouldn't be too tough on him.

In the last hour before midnight, people started to become more and more excited. Bottles of sparkling cider and champagne were brought out, along with yummy desserts that all the volunteer cooks had prepared. Once more, arguments broke out over such things as the perfect recipe for fruit-cake and mince pie.

A hush gradually fell over the room. Jen had been sitting in a soft chair, half-dozing, and she snapped her eyes open, thinking that she'd missed the midnight celebration.

No, it wasn't that. What had stopped the conversation was the appearance of a new guest. Jen dimly recalled meeting him years earlier, and of course she'd seen many photographs of him in her parents' album.

But no one expected to see him tonight. Except Nell. She held out her arms and the man strode across the room to give her a hug. He was dressed in a blue seersucker suit that looked as if it had been slept in for the past fifty or so nights. Papers were sticking out of the pockets of the coat, and there were ink stains—and maybe bloodstains—on the sleeves.

"Chuck, I knew you'd come," Nell said.

"Couldn't miss this party," he replied. Chuck looked at the screen of the laptop, sitting on a table in front of Nell. "I see somebody has put my watch inside a computer."

Jen was going to tell him who did it when another voice boomed out. "Well! Here at last! As usual, you don't bother to let anyone know if you're safe or not."

It was Charley, Chuck's father.

"I didn't know you were worried, Father," said Chuck.

"I wasn't worried, but your mother and Nell were concerned. It just shows what an inconsiderate—"

"Enough!"

Everybody jumped. That had been Nell, using a voice nobody thought a nearly one-hundred-year-old woman could have.

She looked around with fiery eyes. "For the next . . ." She glanced at the ticking watch on the screen. ". . . eleven and a half minutes, there is to be no arguing, accusations, or acrimony. Charley, tell Chuck how delighted you are to see him safe and unharmed."

Pouting, Charley did so.

"And Chuck, tell your father how proud you are of everything he has done."

"Everything?" Chuck was amazed.

"Even the things that you personally would not have done because you are of a different generation," Nell said.

Chuck half-smiled. "Well, when you put it *that* way . . ."

"I do. And while I'm at it, everybody find their family members and tell them you love them, even though you might not understand them."

As everybody shuffled around the room, finding their relatives, Nell went on. "I want to say something else. And whether you listen or not, maybe you'll remember later, after I'm gone."

"We'll be gone by then," said Charley.

Nell ignored him. "Because that's what families are for. They pass things on, one generation to the next, like family heirlooms, or recipes, or stories. Oh, my words and thoughts may not be gold, but they're the best I have to give you. So accept them, add your own to the mix, and pass them on. And you young people? Take care of those memories, because that is all that will be left when we're— whoops, somebody hand me one of those horns. It's almost time."

As the second hand on the laptop watch ticked down, everybody counted with it: "Ten-nine-eight-seven . . ."

After "one" they started to shout "Happy—"

Then the room suddenly went black.

The only light came from the battery-operated laptop screen. The televisions and stereos stopped, and a few people screamed.

"I was right!" Jen could hear Daddy's joyful voice.

Then, just as suddenly, the lights came on again, the televisions flickered to life, and the music started to play again.

High above, on the second-floor landing, Cal stuck his head over the railing. Tran was right behind him, grinning. "Sorry, Dad," said Cal. We flipped the main light switch. Just a joke."

"I can hardly wait to see what happens next," said Nell.

A Few Historical Notes

At the beginning of the 1990s, fewer than 5 percent of American households owned a personal computer. By the end of the decade, the figure was around 50 percent. During that time, the typical home computer increased greatly in speed and memory. However, the operating systems and programs that ran on computers also became larger and more complex. As a result, computer users did not notice much of an actual increase in speed. More complex programs also led to greater numbers of "crashes," in which the computer stopped operating for some reason that was never clearly explained.

Most people didn't seem to mind these glitches, however, and they began to use computers for various tasks and for entertainment. People started with simple things like word processing and spreadsheets and went on to databases or other tasks for home businesses. Game programs became increasingly complex and realistic in their graphics.

The most exciting development in computers for the average user was the Internet. At first it was a way to unify government and university computers in a communications network. Users established bulletin boards in which messages could be exchanged. Then the World Wide Web (WWW) gave the Internet graphics and new, exciting ways to communicate.

Home users started to become part of the Internet by subscribing to service providers like America Online, CompuServe, and others. These services set up chatrooms where members could gather to discuss virtually any issue. Personal messages could also be sent back and forth, both in real time (instant messages) and via e-mail. Virtually every business, large or small, established an e-mail address during the 1990s. (The authors' e-mail address is TandDHoob@aol.com. Write us if you have something to ask or tell us about these books.)

Web sites were almost as popular. These were places on the Internet where an individual person or a business could create their own space that was as complex or simple as they wished. Individuals who subscribed to one of the service providers were often given space for their own Web site as part of the membership fee.

While online, computer users could also log onto games that were played with many other people. The one in this story is strictly the invention of the authors.

As for the Y2K scare, the dire predictions of a global crash did not materialize. Many believe this was due to the preparations made by governments and industry around the world to repair computer systems and make them Y2K compliant. In the United States only a few minor Y2K glitches were reported at the start of 2000.

The Aldrich

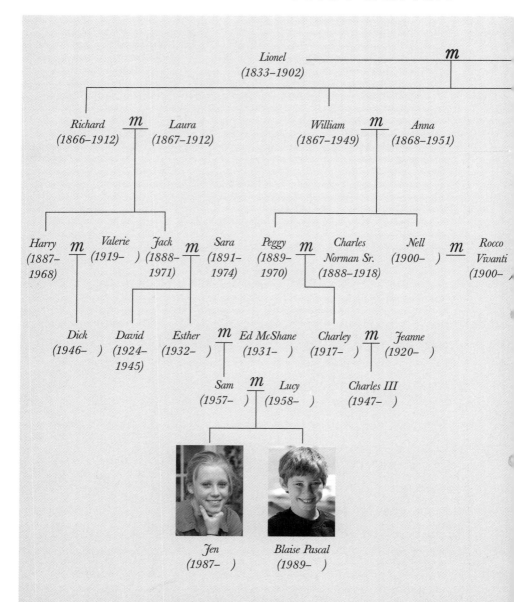

Lionel
(1833–1902) ——————————— *m*

Richard *m* Laura
(1866–1912) (1867–1912)

William *m* Anna
(1867–1949) (1868–1951)

Harry *m* Valerie
(1887– (1919–)
1968)

Jack *m* Sara
(1888– (1891–
1971) 1974)

Peggy *m* Charles
(1889– Norman Sr.
1970) (1888–1918)

Nell *m* Rocco
(1900–) Vivanti
(1900–

Dick David
(1946–) (1924–
1945)

Esther *m* Ed McShane
(1932–) (1931–)

Charley *m* Jeanne
(1917–) (1920–)

Sam *m* Lucy
(1957–) (1958–)

Charles III
(1947–)

Jen
(1987–)

Blaise Pascal
(1989–)

Family

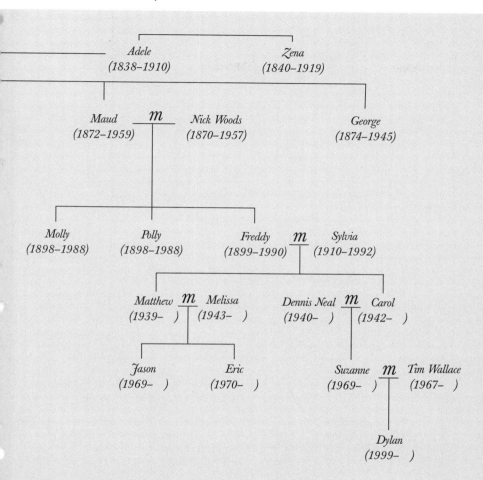

Adele (1838–1910)   Zena (1840–1919)

Maud (1872–1959)   **m**   Nick Woods (1870–1957)   George (1874–1945)

Molly (1898–1988)   Polly (1898–1988)   Freddy (1899–1990)   **m**   Sylvia (1910–1992)

Matthew (1939–)   **m**   Melissa (1943–)   Dennis Neal (1940–)   **m**   Carol (1942–)

Jason (1969–)   Eric (1970–)   Suzanne (1969–)   **m**   Tim Wallace (1967–)

Dylan (1999–)

The Vivanti Family

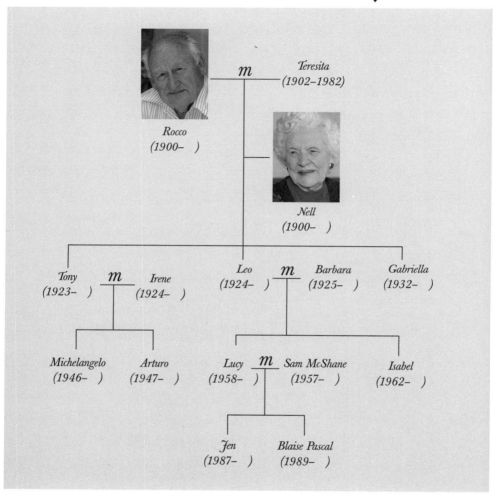

The Dixon Family

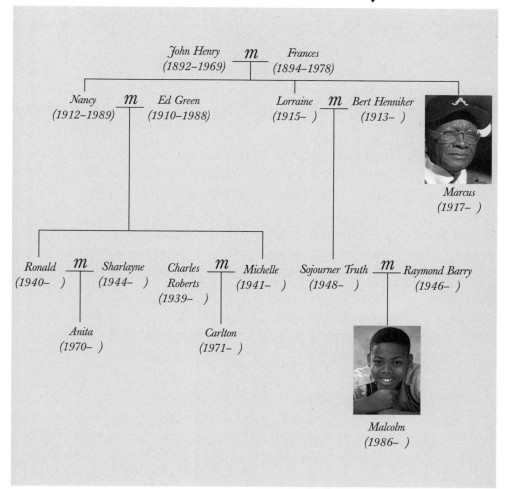

John Henry *m* Frances
(1892–1969) (1894–1978)

Nancy *m* Ed Green
(1912–1989) (1910–1988)

Lorraine *m* Bert Henniker
(1915–) (1913–)

Marcus
(1917–)

Ronald *m* Sharlayne
(1940–) (1944–)

Charles *m* Michelle
Roberts (1941–)
(1939–)

Sojourner Truth *m* Raymond Barry
(1948–) (1946–)

Anita
(1970–)

Carlton
(1971–)

Malcolm
(1986–)

Things That Really Happened

1990

President George H. W. Bush names Dr. Antonia Novello as United States surgeon general. She is both the first female and the first Hispanic to hold that post.

Microsoft releases Windows version 3.0, which becomes the standard operating system for personal computers.

The Human Genome Project, intended to map the entire genetic makeup of human beings, is launched.

After Iraq invades Kuwait, the United States sends military forces to the Persian Gulf in Operation Desert Shield.

1991

In what becomes known as the Persian Gulf War, the United States and its allies defeat Iraq and liberate Kuwait in Operation Desert Storm.

1992

Riots break out in south-central Los Angeles after the acquittal of four white police officers who were recorded on videotape beating Rodney King, a black man they had arrested.

The Mall of America, the biggest shopping center in the United Sates, opens in Bloomington, Minnesota.

Bill Clinton is elected president, defeating President Bush and third-party candidate Ross Perot.

Cellular phones go on sale in the United States; about 10,000 are sold.

During the Years 1990–1999

1993

President Clinton names Janet Reno as the nation's first female attorney general.

A bomb explodes in the parking garage underneath the World Trade Center in New York City. Several Islamic militants are later convicted of planning the attack.

An article in the magazine *Computerworld*, titled "Doomsday 2000," is one of the earliest alerts to the potential Y2K computer problem.

Four federal agents are killed during an unsuccessful raid on the headquarters of the Branch Davidians, a religious group, in Waco, Texas. There followed a 51-day siege of the compound, led by FBI agents. It ended on April 19 when government agents attacked the compound. A fire resulted that killed more than 70 of the men, women, and children inside. The precise cause of the fire was never determined.

1994

On January 1, the North American Free Trade Agreement (NAFTA) takes effect.

Attorney General Janet Reno appoints a special counsel to investigate possible misconduct by President Clinton in Whitewater, an Arkansas real-estate scheme that the president and his wife invested in.

The Republican party wins control of Congress in the November elections.

1995

On April 19, a bomb carried by a truck explodes outside the Murrah Federal Building in Oklahoma City, killing 168 people.

President Clinton signs a bill repealing the 55-mile-an-hour speed limit on federal highways.

When the Republican Congress and President Clinton cannot agree on a budget, the federal government shuts down for six days in November.

1996

A bomb explodes at a military base in Saudi Arabia, killing 19 American soldiers.

President Clinton signs a bill that will end federal subsidies to poor people with children.

President Clinton defeats his Republican opponent, Senator Bob Dole, in the presidential elections. However, the Republicans keep control of both houses of Congress.

Congress passes and President Clinton signs the Communications Decency Act. It is intended to regulate "lewd and obscene" content on the World Wide Web.

1997

Madeleine Albright becomes the first female United States secretary of state.

Tiger Woods, a 21-year-old African-American golfer, wins the prestigious Masters tournament by a record score.

World chess champion Garry Kasparov loses a six-game match to an IBM computer named Deep Blue.

The U.S. Supreme Court declares the Communications Decency Act is an unconstitutional attack on free speech.

The Mattel Company, manufacturer of the Barbie doll, announces that it has made more Barbie dolls (250 million) than the entire population of the United States.

Timothy McVeigh is convicted of conspiracy and murder in the 1995 Oklahoma City bombing, and sentenced to death. Later in the year, Terry Nichols is also convicted on charges related to the bombing.

Representatives from 160 countries meet in Kyoto, Japan, to discuss ways of controlling the climate changes that result from industrial pollution. The delegates agree on a plan to cut so-called "greenhouse gases" by the year 2012. Later, the United States refuses to sign the agreement.

1998

Theodore Kaczynski pleads guilty to mailing bombs to addresses in California and New Jersey. The FBI declares that Kaczynski is the so-called Unabomber, who has been sending bombs through the mail for 20 years.

The movie *Titanic* wins eleven Academy Awards, including best picture of 1997. This ties the record for a single motion picture.

Mark McGuire of the St. Louis Cardinals hits 70 home runs, breaking Roger Maris's single-season record. Sammy Sosa of the Chicago Cubs also breaks Maris's record, with a season total of 66.

Kenneth Starr, special prosecutor for the Whitewater scandals, sends a report to Congress stating that President Clinton had a sexual relationship with a Congressional intern, Monica Lewinsky. The Republican-controlled House of Representatives impeaches Clinton on counts of perjury and obstruction of justice, because he lied to a grand jury about the affair.

1999

President Clinton is tried before the Senate on the charges brought by the House. A two-thirds vote of senators is necessary to convict. One count of perjury gains only 45 votes, out of 100 senators; the obstruction of justice vote gains 50 votes, still short of the two-thirds majority, so President Clinton remains in office.

Two students at Columbine High School in Littleton, Colorado, shoot and kill 12 other students and a teacher, before killing themselves. This is the deadliest of several school shootings by students during the decade.

The Dow Jones Industrial Index, a benchmark of stock market prices, reaches 10,000 for the first time.

John F. Kennedy Jr., son of the former president, is killed with his wife and sister-in-law in the crash of a small plane that Kennedy was piloting.